Acclaim for

This is a riveting tale of betrayal, deceit, seduction, lust, legal drama, revenge, power and money. I felt like I knew all the characters personally and knew all the places where the events took place. I couldn't put down the book once I started reading it. Kanayo O. Kanayo and Tony Ekwoaba have written a brilliant thriller that I hope will be turned into a film soon.

— Dr Joe Abah

The central theme of this work of fiction is on the niggling social issue of will - whether testate or intestate. What is really constructive in this genre of legal fiction, however, is the creative form in which it is narrated. In what is truly a masterpiece, the authors have weaved an enthralling story around a solemn topic that is as educative as it is entertaining— that too in a most intriguing, captivating and gripping manner. The style and diction are simple enough to elucidate the workings of Nigeria's justice system and, by extension, some aspects of the daily life of the ordinary man on the streets of Nigeria. This work is a collector's item that ought to feature on every family shelf.

— John C. Azu, Judicial Editor for Daily Trust Newspaper and media ambassador of the African Court on Human and Peoples Rights

The Testator grips you on page one and doesn't let go until the breathless ending. Together, Kanayo and Ekwoaba have created a three-dimensional world filled with innocence and greed, life and murder.

— Mary Harris, US Author and editor

This is a wonderful work of art that is just as entertaining as it is didactic...There is an ample deployment of legal registers for students studying or taking courses in English language and easily passes for an introductory course in a law degree programme...

— His Worship, Samuel Ebiyekhimi Idhiarhi,
Chief Magistrate, FCT, Abuja.

The authors have demonstrated that they possess the requisite expertise and gravitas to churn out this historic masterpiece of literary work. Exquisite, superb, and piercingly engaging, you won't dare put the book down until the last page. *The Testator* is a thrilling socio-legal piece that dares your imagination and creativity.

— Chief Mike Ozekhome, SAN, OFR, Ph.D.

With lush, breathtaking prose, this fast-moving legal thriller delivers an intriguing portrayal of crime, family, culture, economic anxiety, and the ways in which people navigate a broken system. An incisive political commentary with unforgettable characters and an enthralling series of events, *The Testator* makes for both an exciting and intellectual read.

— Jake Okechukwu Effoduh, Partner, Praxis & Gnosis Law,
Nigeria; Vanier Scholar, Osgoode Hall Law School, Canada.

This fictional thriller, The Testator depicts the ups and downs of legal practice. It reveals the intersections of law, life, criminality and the triumph of justice with the aid of technology. It is a masterpiece on the beauty of art and law. Kudos to the inventive genius of the authors.

— *Prof. Yemi Akinseye-George, SAN*

"In the TESTATOR, the authors take the readers through a surreal and magical adventure in the tragicomedy of power, law and human suffering. This tale has a dramatic effect; it runs like a real theater of the absurd and malevolence interspersed with exhilarating dark humors. The plots are a tightly woven tale that reads like something from Albert Camus's The Trial. Its twists and turns are cinematic. As I read, I could imagine myself with a cup of popcorn trapped in the sight and sound of a big cinema screen. The Testator marries uncanny insights about the pathology of the criminal justice system with a cynical appreciation of the human condition. Intrigues, greed and fear are woven together in a tapestry of maladministration of justice. Shakespeare would find so much to laugh about in the book. He thought all lawyers should be killed. After reading this book, he may now say :"First, let's kill the human'. Kanayo and Ekwoaba's book deserve another and another read. It is worth the time."

— *Dr Sam Amadi, Associate Professor and Director of Abuja School of Social and Political Thought*

In this interesting work of fiction that marries law with romance, betrayal, comedy and terror, ace actor, Kanayo O. Kanayo, and Tony Ekwoaba, deploy a theme that is fresh and resonant yet hardly ever discussed in a society where many prefer to live in denial about the certainty of death. Beautifully written and enjoyable from the first page to the last, 'The Testator' is one of those imaginative and gripping tales so authentic that readers begin to ask: Is it based on real life experience?

—Olusegun Adeniyi, Chairman, THISDAY Editorial Board

"The Testator is a masterpiece! The authors' imagination and prowess in writing captures the mind from start to finish."

—Saifullah I. U. Bello Esq.

"In The Testator, Kanayo O Kanayo and Tony Ekwoaba have masterfully delivered a gripping legal thriller full of twists, turns, suspense, drama and compelling characters. From the first chapter, you enter a world of despondency and reincarnation. By the time you are done, you are filled with rage and relief."

—Simon Kolawole, journalist and founder of
The Cable online newspaper

THE TESTATOR

A LEGAL THRILLER

KANAYO O. KANAYO

TONY EKWOABA

THE TESTATOR

Copyright © 2021 Kanayo O. Kanayo and Tony Ekwoaba

ALL RIGHTS RESERVED

Harmony Publishing
Plot 1 Emmanuel Anabor, Off Mopo Road, United Estate,
Sangotedo,
Lagos, Nigeria
+2347032212481
publish@harmonypublishing.com.ng

ISBN-13: 978-100-52145-3-1

Edited by Tope-EniObanke Adegoke and Mary Harris
Book Cover Design by Samuel Anwakang
Formated by Eswari Kamireddy

Dedication

The book is dedicated to every lover of justice. We pray for a better justice delivery system in our beloved country Nigeria.

FOREWORD

The certainty of death strongly suggests that man should by all means possible prepare for what is to happen to his Estate upon his demise. The said suggestion was well taken by the billionaire and business mogul, Chief Peter Onu as captured in the riveting prose which is befittingly titled 'The Testator'.

Upon reading the manuscript of 'The Testator' which was presented to me by the authors: His Worship, Tony Ekwoaba and the Veteran actor and Lawyer, Kanayo O. Kanayo. Esq., MFR., I must say that I find the work to be a masterpiece and its theme moved me to graciously accept to write this foreword.

Although 'The Testator' is a fictional literary work, same mirrors the real life quagmires and theatrics enveloping the issue of inheriting the deceased member of a family. The work also exhibits the advantages of writing a Will. One of such advantage being to prevent one's kindred from engaging in lifelong family feud over one's Estate long after one's demise.

In 'The Testator', Chief Peter Onu foresaw the war that would have ruined his empire and he proactively arrested same using his testamentary directives. Other advantages of a Will as exposed in the captivating prose includes giving the testator: the leverage of appointing Executors to distribute his assets; the ability to appoint specific persons to manage his business; the freedom to make donation to charitable organizations of his choice; being assured of unbroken chain of administration of his Estate and the chance to give directions as to how he wishes to be buried.

Being a judicial officer, I must commend the effort of the authors in exposing several aspect of the legal system particularly the hint at the practice of the legal profession by young lawyers; the proceeding of the court system, the administration of criminal justice and the prison system. All of which encapsulates the apprehension of the citizens as manifested through the various characters in the instant narrative. I also commend the authors' effort at using a fictional tale to bring about an appraisal and a critique of the socio-economic and socio-cultural issues prevalent in Nigeria.

Above all, 'The Testator' will serve every reader with an effortless assortment of imaginative entertainment, legal education and socio-cultural lessons owing to the intrigues in the plots, the clarity of information supplied, the richness in proverbial quotes and the vivid description of the setting.

I heartily recommend 'The Testator' for every household and every individual from all works of life and I can confidently say that once you open the first page, you will find it difficult to resist flipping the next page till you get to the end.

HON. JUSTICE BENEDICT BAKWAPH KANYIP (FNIALS)
President, National Industrial Court of Nigeria

CHAPTER 1

Pius leaned on the big mahogany table that used to be the office front desk. He'd just been wondering how he would accomplish the day's tasks without a secretary. Rebecca Ocholi, his secretary who was the last staff member on that desk, had just resigned yesterday. She simply sent a text message that she had gotten a job elsewhere. This was after five months of not being paid any salary, five months of her coming to work, hoping things would get better, but things never did.

At past 8 o'clock, her usual time of resumption, she was nowhere around the office. Pius was reluctant to call. You know that moment you wished to scold someone but you couldn't because you weren't meeting your part of the deal, so you just accepted whatever you got? It was like a child hurt in his disobedience holding back his tears. That was what was happening with Pius. She was conscientious. One amongst a dozen of them that had come in the hope that things would get better; but as they say, boiling a rotten egg for hours would never undo its rottenness.

On the peeling wall was a framed picture of Pius with Mr Olasupo Shasore, SAN, a former Attorney General of Lagos State. Pius wore an elaborate, expensive wig and gown. Strangely, it was the same wig and gown he's had to date, though it just didn't feel the same anymore, as though the glamour evaporated with the fall. But how did he get so messed, so damned messed up. He has asked himself this question a billion times and more, and perhaps he would keep asking for the rest of his life.

His thoughts were interrupted by footsteps approaching the staircase. The two offices on the top floor were closed. They usually closed early before 6:00 pm. He looked in the direction of a wall clock, it read 3:00 pm. It was in a state of comatose, static. He recalled the last time Rebecca had requested money for stationeries and batteries for the clocks and he had told her he would give her the next day. He never did. He checked his Michael Kors wristwatch and it read 6:21 pm. Whoever it was wasn't going to the office above him. The person was coming to his law office.

Pius listened as the footsteps approached.

The only visitor he has had in recent times was Michael, the house agent. He had come innumerable times asking for the rent and had threatened to evict him. He'd spoken about the rent perhaps in every language he could speak, and was determined to get his pound of flesh, if it came to that. It wasn't just the rent. Pius hadn't been quite diligent with all the other payments, including electricity bill, security and waste disposal bills. Michael had seen for himself how bad it looked, even though he disbelieved it, as nobody would think a lawyer of Pius' status couldn't afford to pay even electricity bills which the tailors downstairs paid ad libitum. It sort of lent to the stereotype that lawyers would rather make trouble than pay rent. Whatever it was going on, Michael had said, he wouldn't keep up with Pius' excuses for long. He was fed up!

Each approaching footsteps doubled Pius' heartbeat. It didn't sound like Michael's. He'd just been around yesterday, when he threatened rather subtly that things would be different the next time he came around. He didn't have to say it; Pius knew. He knew that Michael liked him no more than a dog liked a cat.

The footsteps drew closer, slowly and laboriously.

"Could it be a client?" Pius soliloquized, not sure what else to think. He hasn't had any in months, as far as he could recollect, except for the few cases that brought the few pennies here and there, most of whom were from a few old clients who didn't bother finding out where he was hiding; none of them cared to visit the rathole he called an office as if they knew it wasn't worth their visit.

Whoever it was kept climbing, and he listened. It seemed the person hummed as he or she came up the stairs, even though he barely heard anything due to the noise outside. Whoever it was surely was as heavy as the steps that came pounding on the stairs.

Then there was a rattle on his office door. Pius quickly stood upright and stepped away from the mahogany table. He made for the door. But before his hand could reach the handle, the door swung open.

The man standing in the doorway looked no less than the trunk of an iroko tree. He filled the entire doorway. He was as tall as he was broad, with little eyes that flashed from his ball-round face. A curly moustache rested beneath his flat, thick nose. He must have been in his fifties, and no less. He wore a black, expensive-looking coat.

"Barrister Pius?" His voice was hoarse and loud. As he spoke, he panted, and Pius noticed it was quite a task for him to climb the stairs.

Pius nodded.

"Barrister Pius Egbe?"

He nodded again.

The heavy figure moved farther into the room and stretched

out a thick arm for a handshake. His grip was firm, his palm wrapped around Pius'.

"You can call me Nick," he said. Pius caught a whiff of cigar in his breath.

He glanced at him, not sure what he could possibly do for such a figure.

"Won't you take me into your office?" Nick roared.

"Oh, yes! Yes!" Pius exclaimed, recovering from his absent-mindedness. He'd been so stunned at the figure before him that he forgot to take him into the office. He turned and led the way.

It was a small law office. Front desk, a small shelf nailed to the wall for a library, the Principal's office, and a workstation for two lawyers. The office was mostly partitioned with board and glass. The previous occupant did the partitioning before the law firm was set up. Pius only retained the earlier partitioning and repainted the place.

Nick looked through the spaces as they walked through the passageway, examining everything with rapt attention. He didn't utter a word until he got to a small cubicle with the tag, Principal's Office.

"How long have you been here?" he asked.

"Three years."

"Since the fall," Nick stated. It wasn't a question. It was a re-mark, one that dripped with sarcasm.

Both men walked into the Principal's Office. There, at the centre, was a big desk, with two chairs for visitors. Pius crossed over and sat down.

The visitors' chairs hadn't had anyone sit on them for aeons. Apart from the chairs, there was a bookshelf filled with a few law books, law reports, and dusty case files. The entire place reeked of musty papers.

"You may have a seat," Pius stated, noticing that Nick was still standing. He was looking at the framed pictures on the peeled wall, old pictures of the Principal with top lawyers, politicians, and businessmen. Those were the days when Pius Egbe was a name that commanded respect. Those days he had dreamed someday he would reach the apogee of his career, that he would become a Senior Advocate of Nigeria, and he was close to some of the requirements: ten years post call to bar, eight judgements in the High Court, six Court of Appeal and three Supreme Court judgements, receipts of his practicing fees payment.

"Sit down, you said?" Nick asked, rather amused. Pius noticed his reluctance. The chair was very dusty and dirty. He grabbed a piece of cloth and dusted the chair and beckoned Nick to sit. Nick sat down and both men laughed.

"Mr Nick. How may I help you?" Pius asked in the most professional tone, trying as much as he could to be polite and welcoming. He wouldn't miss this single client who went through the stress of finding him in the rat hole he called an office. The gold Rolex watch on his fat wrist and big ring on his finger showed he wasn't a man of mean earnings. His coat really didn't look good, it was a horrible taste in fashion, but the wristwatch and ring were a statement. A statement to the fact that he was a rich man. A very rich man.

"How may you help me?" he asked. He seemed to have this habit of replying to things with questions. Pius didn't know why the big man did that, but he responded with a smile, still trying to sound polite.

Back in law school, students had dreams of changing the world once they became lawyers. They were taught how to welcome clients in some course called Client Counselling - Treat Clients as Kings: make them comfortable when they visit your law office, offer them drinks, coffee or tea, ask them, "Hope it wasn't difficult finding my office?", and if they were feeling hot, and all that sort of questions.

With experience, Pius had learnt it didn't really matter. A client not poised to hire you wouldn't, no matter how you tried to please him.

Whatever brought this big man to his office must be serious. He seemingly needed help, but he was blissfully unaware that Pius needed him more.

A moment of silence followed, and then Nick began to tap his finger on the table. Then he started on what appeared like a tale.

"I've been following your story," he began. "You are quite a character they say, smart and tricky." He smiled and went on in his hoarse voice. "You have brains, they say, and you're reckless, but you have guts." He looked at Pius as though to verify this. Pius remained quiet and listened.

"Rumour has it that as a young man, you took risks and made a good fortune. But then as a man with a penchant for risk-taking, you also lost the fortune by taking more risks." He smiled sheepishly as he said this.

"You also got into trouble, some deep trouble, but as a tricky guy, you got yourself out of it, or at least some of it." His tiny eyes probed Pius, who'd noticed this and tried to not give himself away with his expression.

"When things became messy, you disappeared from your circle, you ran and hid yourself in this dungeon. You set this place up with the crumbs that fell from your hallowed table. Hired a few lawyers and stayed low key. You only took cases from magistrate courts and nobody in this environment knows who you were. Again, rumour had it that you burnt yourself in the car, some said they saw you die and all sorts of stories. But till this time, no one knows exactly which is true."

"What rumours?" Pius asked, believing he had to say something.

"You know, the tales in the circles. It all died down eventually, and people went about their business."

Pius shook his head, still wondering where the big man was going with all this.

"And like in recent times, luck always ran out on you. Even this hasn't worked," he intoned, taking in the office with disgust evident on his face.

"You haven't paid your staff, nor your rent. The landlord is threatening to throw you out any moment."

"You have been following me?" Pius said, infuriated that the man knew so much about him.

"I said that from the beginning. Not that I had been following you, but we had to know enough to decide if you were the man we wanted for the job," he said as though it was some achievement.

"You are afraid of how to and what would become of you when you quit. You have no child, no wife, and nothing really matters anymore. The glamourous girls that sucked on your life in those good days have all deserted you upon your fall."

"Enough!" Pius shouted, in a weak attempt to ease the humiliation he felt. "What do you want from me?"

It was obvious the man had done his investigations. Though he was fat and ugly, he wasn't stupid. He was sharp-witted and scheming, maybe more tricky than one would ever find out. Something about him hinted at trouble.

"I have a job for you." He flashed the thick ring and gold Rolex watch at Pius.

"What kind of job?" Pius inquired. He was convinced it couldn't be anything to do with the courts. Such a man didn't use lawyers, and if he did, not his kind of lawyers. He was the type who took care of his problems the street way.

"It's a job you alone can do. The kind that would be believed if you did it." He stroked his moustache and focused on Pius as he said this.

"Why me?"

"Because you are a perfect match for the job." As he said this, he put his hand in one of the pockets of his coat and brought out a bundle of dollar bills. They were neatly piled together; you could easily notice there was more from where it came. He dropped the bundle on the table.

The rush of adrenaline that came with sight of those bills tripled Pius' heartbeat. The frontal lobe of his brain was already thinking of the problems the money could solve. He couldn't take his eyes off Benjamin Franklin on the hundred-dollar notes.

"This is a teaser for you!" he said, trying to lure him further. He'd seen the greed and how much Pius wished to grab the bills and turn them from one side of the table to the other.

"Barrister Pius, you can have this and much more if you agree to do this simple task. Chief Onu is dead, and all we are asking is for you to read his will!" he said calmly, and examined the re-action that came with that.

Pius sank into his seat, thrown off by the statement.

"Chief Onu? Chief Peter Onu? He definitely can't be dead. Why would you pay so much for me to read his will? He's not dead, and how can I be sure of what you are saying? I spoke with him two days ago,"

"Chief is dead, even though it's not been made public yet. He died yesterday. Call his wife, Mrs Jennifer, if you doubt me. She's aware of this meeting."

Pius paused to turn this over in his mind for a while. The woman wasn't a good person. She was nasty and cared more about her skin and looks than anyone else. He was Chief's personal lawyer for years, until things took a bad turn for him and Chief Onu had told him to be wary of her. Chief Onu made every public show of affection towards her and acted as though his marriage to her was beautiful, but he had secretly complained that marrying her was a grave mistake. Poor man. He had all the wealth but never had true peace of mind.

"What is the money for?" Pius asked, knowing very well the woman wasn't that generous. She could only offer this if she had something up her sleeves, he thought.

"For your logistics, wardrobe, and other things," he said sternly. "There are a lot of eyes on the will and there will be some fighting to do. You need that for the job."

"I will put a call across to Madam," Pius stated.

"You do whatever you wish, but please note that you leave tomorrow afternoon for Abuja," Nick said as he made to leave.

"The money? You are leaving the money? I haven't told you if I'm taking the job or not."

"Do you have a choice? You are Chief's personal lawyer, you have to perform your final respect by helping to read and perfect his will."

"But he didn't tell me he had a will," Pius contested.

"He didn't?" Nick asked, expressing surprise, but then continued. "He didn't have to tell you. He may have mentioned it but it's the old man's right to make his will however he wished. Isn't it, Barrister?"

Pius didn't say anything as he stood to watch the man leave.

"The money is for your clothing; you look horrible. Change and get ready. Your flight ticket will be sent to you. Your flight is at twelve noon tomorrow."

CHAPTER 2

A black Toyota Corolla cruised around in search of a parking space. The street had lots of offices and was busy vehicular and human traffic. The road was narrow and one would have to be careful to avoid getting his car scraped by other drivers.

Tim Akpan was looking exasperated already. He'd had a frustrating day in court and didn't want any further stress.

"Why do these idiots just block the road, these Abuja taxis, all they look out for are passengers rather than other road users. Gush!" He voiced his frustration.

After about twenty minutes, he found a spot. It was as though someone had just driven out of the place, creating a space he could squeeze his Toyota Corolla into. He would spend just a few minutes, he thought, then run back to his office.

About the time he left the court, he'd received a call from a renowned detective friend of his who had often referred cases to him over the years. Detective Chris had said there was an important matter he would have him handle. The kind of case that would liberate him from years of work without commensurate pay.

"Tim, this is a lifetime opportunity you can't reject." He'd sounded rather urgent over the phone.

Tim stepped out of the car, taking his suit that he hung on the headrest. He wore the faded suit and opened the back door to grab his diary and a pen. He may need to jot down some things at the meeting. The rear seat of his car was jammed with books, case files, and law reports. This was the life of a hungry defence lawyer. Perhaps this case would give him the break he needed desperately.

He removed his bib and unfastened his stud, loosening his collar because he could barely breathe. He threw the bib on the rear seat and slammed the door.

The environment looked busy, though everyone minded their business. It didn't seem like anyone noticed him as he slid the key in its hole and turned its lock. Again, he looked over his shoulder to check that no one was looking. He was glad no one was looking. The car was old, a little old for a five-years-post-call lawyer like himself. He had to turn the key several times before it locked. He wished it had a remote lock, so he could step away and press a button like other car owners did. He'd been told by his mechanic that it was possible, but the amount he mentioned could as well pay for his brief writing training. He spent the money on the latter.

Detective Chris's office was on the fourth floor of Metro Plaza. Tim passed a few blocks before he got to the Plaza. The elevator wasn't working, and when he asked a uniformed security guard at the entrance, he was told there was a power outage. The elevator worked only with the central power. He took the stairs.

Detective Chris was expecting him when he got to his office.

"Let him in." Chris yelled at his staff once he saw Tim.

"Welcome, Tim. Please sit down." He motioned to Tim and went over to sit at the other end of the table. The office was well furnished with expensive leather chairs, some art decoration, and a pile of security books on a shelf. Framed images of Chris with some important personalities and a closed circuit television screen hung on the wall.

Chris was a short, spare guy, in his middle forties. He was the type that didn't make any impression when you first met him, but would distil so much information from you before you knew it. If you weren't told the nature of his work, you wouldn't make the right guess. He looked frail and unassuming.

They had been friends for over two decades. They had run into each other one night as Chris had gone to study at the law facility.

"You've remodelled this place. It's so different from the last time I was here," Tim said as he looked around the beautiful office.

"Thank you. You haven't visited much," Chris stated.

"I've been busy with cases. It's been my busiest year, with nothing to show for it though."

"That's about to change!" Chris opened a drawer and brought out a folder.

"Tell me more."

"Does the name Chief Peter Onu ring a bell?" Chris asked, looking intently at Tim.

"Chris, who doesn't know Chief Onu? The billionaire oil mogul and owner of Onu Group of companies."

"He died this morning."

"How? I don't understand. Wasn't he on Channels TV last week talking about the acquisition of some massive land for a real estate project? Are you sure this information is right?"

"It's very accurate. I'm well informed by my source. The truth is that the family, or rather his wife, doesn't want anyone to know. But as we speak, Chief Onu is in the morgue."

"That's sad," Tim stated, surprised and amused at the same time.

"So how do I come in? I'm not the police or a detective like you, if it is about the cause of his death."

"Do you know this boy? I suppose you represent him?" Chris asked as he handed over a picture he'd taken out from the folder to Tim.

"Yes. That's Emeka Okoromadu, my client. He is a security guard at one of Chief's engineering yards," Tim said, not sure whether to say anything else. He didn't know how much Chris knew and it wasn't incumbent on him to state the nature of the offence the boy was charged with and if the boy was accused of murdering the old man. He was ready to cooperate with Chris, but he wasn't going to reveal much that would go against client confidentiality. The hearts of lawyers are choked with secrets, secrets of clients they must not divulge no matter how weighty it seemed, and the rules of professional conduct of lawyers forbade them.

"Isn't he the one you are representing in respect to an allegation of theft at the engineering yards?" Chris asked.

"Yes, but the young man is innocent. I have evidence to establish this."

"Where is he now?"

"He was arraigned two days ago. We haven't been able to perfect his bail, so he's in prison. If you think the guy killed Chief, he's got a strong alibi. The boy was in prison when Chief died."

"Who is alleging that he killed Chief? Chief was, in fact, his father." Chris said calmly and watched Tim react like someone who'd just seen a ghost.

"His father? What do you mean?"

"Three months ago, I got a call from a man who introduced himself as Chief Onu." Chris raised his right hands to his mouth, then rubbed his palm on his face.

"At first I didn't believe it was him," he continued, "not that

I didn't sense it from his soft, calm voice, but I wasn't sure the billionaire would call me. I knew whatever made him call me was certainly serious. He pleaded anonymity and agreed to meet with me at a certain discreet location to talk. He said he had done his research and was told I knew my job, and he wasn't expecting anything less from me than excellent work."

Chris looked, glad to see Tim was listening.

"The meeting was arranged, discreetly though, and we met at one of the presidential suites at Hilton. He and I were alone. He asked the security detail with him to move out of sight and hearing.

Tim looked up and their eyes met.

"He told me he was being blackmailed. That a certain woman he had run into many years ago suddenly resurfaced and had been disturbing him, saying that she had a child for him. She said that she was going to expose him and run to the media if he didn't do something about the child. He said he didn't have an issue with taking care of the young man; in fact, he would be the happiest person on earth if indeed he did have such a son, but he needed to find out if truly the young man was his child. He asked the best way this could be confirmed. I told him to run a DNA test on the boy. He gave me the image of the boy and some other details about him."

"Did you find out?" Tim asked, wishing it was true.

"I did." Chris smiled. "And my investigation revealed that the boy worked as a security guard in one of Chief's engineering yards. I didn't know much about him, and how to go about this without raising red flags that could turn up to cause some damage to Chief. I also didn't want to raise the young man's hopes or expose him to facts that could make him start feeling entitled to Chief's property, so I got someone to get me his hair strand for a DNA. I actually paid two persons, his friend and his barber. I didn't let them know what it was for, though. The results, when run by two reputable lab centres, came out positive. The young man is Chief's son."

"Did you tell Chief your finding before he died?"

"Yes, I did. We were both making inquiries about the boy when I discovered he was being arraigned for a criminal act. I wanted to find out more before letting Chief know, and when I discovered you were in the matter, I said I should call you."

"Chief planned to call a meeting with his family, to introduce the boy as his son. He had informed me about this and was intending to do so next week, only for me to hear he's dead."

"How did you find out about his death?"

"I called his number; it rang but he didn't answer it, and after a while the phone was switched off. I had to contact my source, who then informed me that Chief had just died and had been taken to the morgue. The truth is that I had tipped the gate man in a compound next to Chief's. The Fulani man made friends with the Hausa security guard at Chief's House. The Fulani man told me his friend had told him his *Oga* had just died, and that he doesn't trust the wife, who he said is wicked and might chase him away. He begged my source, that is, his Fulani friend, that if Chief's wife drives him away, he would stay with him a few nights before he could get a place. They took the corpse out very early, but my source said he saw the ambulance leave."

"That is pathetic. How do we go about this?"

"We will have to come up with a plan. But you must know that the wife is a fierce woman. She will be ready to fight. I also heard that Chief has a grown daughter from his first marriage. I need to find out more about the girl. You do your homework on the boy. What does he need to get his bail perfected?"

"He needs two sureties who are Government officers of Grade Level Fifteen and someone with landed property. I'm not accustomed to getting paid sureties for clients. I don't know how to do that. I wish this was in Lagos where there are bondsmen. If only Abuja courts would introduce the scheme."

"I will get a few people I've worked with to help. But don't you think the boy is safer in prison? I know the family we are dealing with. They are dangerous."

"If you can get the sureties ready, we'll get him out and then we will worry about his safety. If they are that dangerous, as you say, I don't suggest he stay in the prison either. It's better if we get him to a safe house, or get him out of town."

"Chief Onu is worth billions. His wife would do anything to get anyone out of the way. I want you to talk to the boy. Let him understand the dangers ahead and be prepared for war. I don't know if Chief left any will. We will find out about that," Chris stated, slightly authoritative. He was older in age than Tim, so he took advantage of Tim's non-egoistic posture as a lawyer. Tim was so simple; he didn't like being addressed as "barrister". He would often say that "barrister" is not a title.

"Would you find out about his death? He may have been murdered." Tim asked.

"I can, but that shouldn't be our focus now. Our aim is to get this boy his share in the man's fortune and get our cut from it. You have to convince him that it's worth the fight. Have you seen his mother?"

"I haven't heard about her. He never mentioned her."

"We need to find her. That woman must be some hard nut, considering the worrisome look on Chief's face when we met. She has to be brought into this."

"Okay then, I will get to the boy. Let's meet again in a few days as things unfold."

Chris thanked Tim for coming and saw him to the door.

***

Tim stepped out of the meeting, enthusiastic about a promising future. He'd taken the boy's case without expecting much and when the boy couldn't pay him, he'd decided to do the case pro bono. After all, he had always wished to approach the Legal Aid Council to get briefs of indigent persons, but his commitment at the office wouldn't let him. Who would think that Emeka the guard was heir to Chief Onu's wealth? And the boy wasn't even aware of this. It was like someone in a pool of water while soap lather burned his eyes. He must see the boy urgently, he thought, despite the growing pile of tasks that demanded his attention from his seniors at the office. He wouldn't miss this great opportunity.

He stepped out of the plaza. The street was as busy when he arrived. He quickened his pace towards where he parked his car, while these thoughts ran through his mind. What was on his mind was to get home, take a bath, eat, and come up with a plan to see Emeka at Kuje prison. He hurried up to where he'd parked his car.

The car wasn't there!

The damn Toyota Corolla, 2009 model, black colour, wasn't where he left it.

Tim froze. Dozen things ran through his mind. Where would he start from without a car and his case files in the car? How on earth would he start all over on the cases? The evidence and exhibits were all gone. There were over twenty case files in the car.

A colleague had once told him not to put those case files in his car, that it was dangerous. He didn't see the danger in it. It was his car and he didn't lend it to anyone. Keeping those files in the office really wasn't smart. He didn't want his principal to notice his private practice, on the side; he wouldn't approve of it. Most seniors, mostly Senior Advocates, pay other lawyers peanuts, yet some wouldn't let you grow. They felt since they pay you, they own you. You had to handle whatever personal brief you got in secret, and you couldn't resign, because you needed their office for the research, library, and the feel of an office.

He looked around for who to ask, muttering, "But it was here. I mean, I parked the car here, like this," gesturing how he parked the car.

"Excuse me, please, did you see the car I just parked here?" he asked a passerby.

"I didn't," the lady responded and continued, visibly angry over the seemingly stupid question she'd been asked.

"Excuse me, I parked my car here a while ago, did you see anyone move it?" he asked another lady running point of sale business under an umbrella.

"I didn't. Sorry!" She continued what she was doing.

Tim could no longer hold it in. It was like some nightmare you wished had never happened. He removed his suit jacket, threw it on the sidewalk, and screamed.

"Oh God! My car has been stolen. My car, my life! All my practice books, materials, and clients' case files, gone. I'm finished." He sobbed.

People gathered around, some to inquire, some to console him, but none of that mattered anymore. The car was gone.

He had to inform Chris, he thought. He started running towards Chris's office. Surprised at his sudden pace, some of the men in the crowd that had gathered ran after him, believing he had gone mad and might hurt himself.

CHAPTER 3

The phone rang as Mrs Jennifer was about to step into the Jacuzzi. She'd switched off her MTN line so she wouldn't get any further calls from people who couldn't reach Chief. She wasn't ready to talk about his demise to anyone, and she'd turned his phone off as well. Her Airtel line was known only by a handful of people, so she left that on. When it rang, she knew she had to take it.

She dropped the scrub in the sink and quickly went to take the call.

"Hello, Ma, the job has been done," Nick's hoarse voice sounded on the other end.

"He agreed to come? Tell me more." She sat on the toilet seat.

"He agreed after I spoke to him," Nick stated as though it was all by his efforts alone.

"He didn't take the money?" Jennifer asked, anxious to learn the magic Nick did that the money couldn't do.

"He did," Nick admitted.

"That means he needed it so dearly. What was his reaction when you told him Chief was dead?"

"He didn't believe it, but he said he would call you."

"And the Will? Did he know about it?"

"He wasn't aware of any Will. In fact, he said Chief didn't tell him about any Will. Do you think we should still use him?"

"Don't believe what he says; lawyers are economical with the truth. I don't want to take chances. If there's another Will he's hiding, I want to know and if there isn't, I still prefer him reading the Will we have. He was his lawyer, after all."

"Yes, Madam. I agree."

There was a drawn silence on both ends for a while.

"He said he will call you. Did he try reaching out to you?" Nick broke the silence.

"He may have called, but you know the MTN line is off. I called him though to speak with him, but it was brief." It was indeed brief. When Jennifer called, her conversation with Barrister Pius was brief. There was nothing more than the consolations from one end and receipt of the same from the other. Each knew they didn't like the other, and Jennifer acted well enough as someone in grief. Pius knew well it was all pretence. He agreed to meet her soon when he came to Abuja and that was it.

"Nick, get into Abuja tomorrow," she said. "I have work for you." She dropped the call. He'd been one of her errand dogs, getting all sorts of dirty deals done for her without a word.

Jennifer picked up the scrub and stepped into the Jacuzzi. She lay on her back, stroked the soapy water while thoughts swam in her mind. Her eyes closed.

It doesn't feel like I just became a widow, she thought. The old man had been dead all along. He hadn't been useful for anything, other than his money. He was too old and too busy to love a woman. "I didn't know why I stayed in the marriage this long," she muttered.

***

Emeka Okoromadu woke up in prison, wishing daybreak hadn't come. At night, he was afraid to close his eyes, as much as he was terrified to open them as dawn approached. He wasn't sure which was more unsettling, the fear of what might happen to him while he slept or the trauma that followed when he woke up. Such was the anxiety characterized prison life!

He'd heard about prisons, but he'd never anticipated he would be locked up in one someday. He had tried to live an upright and cautious lifestyle – what you might call an honest life. Or rather, so he thought, until this incident that changed everything. Before then, he'd never been to a police station nor had any issue that warranted police involvement. And he didn't know what the courts looked like. Lo and behold, the events of the preceding weeks had taught him that one could not truly be too careful to stay out of trouble. Sometimes, trouble came calling, clothed in beautiful attire; you would never know.

Emeka released a sigh, he couldn't help but flash back to how it had all started.

That hot afternoon, the garbage man had walked by, shouting *"Bola, bola,"* asking for iron scraps.

"…anything not used, anything not needed, anything not useful," he called out as he pushed his truck, filled with rusty irons, to the gate post. On that day, Emeka was the security guard on duty. There were two guards, but Tunde had gone into the yard to defecate. He'd been eating and stooling all day. The man could eat just about anything. Emeka would marvel at how much he consumed and how he could sustain his eating habit. He wasn't steady at the post; again, he'd excused himself to fill his fat belly and stool afterwards. Emeka had thought of chasing the garbage man away, but then he felt it wouldn't cost him anything to help the young man. After all, the bolts and rusty irons littered the yard everywhere, causing car tires to rupture. He told himself he would help the man. So as the garbage man sought his help, he let him into the compound to fetch the irons and bolts while he watched. The man took as many as he could and thanked him. He also thanked Tunde who'd just joined them from inside. Unbeknownst to Emeka, his act of generosity would boomerang, letting loose the monster that would eventually consume him. The garbage man, upon seeing the stored facilities in the yard – wires, irons, electrical materials — began nurturing the intent of getting more, and he was glad to connive with anyone to obtain those things. All he needed was someone in need of something he had, and Tunde was the perfect match.

Over the past weeks, Tunde arranged to give out company properties to the garbage guy in exchange for payments from him. He made it seem as though he and Emeka were in the business together. They'd begun with the little things, but the garbage guy got greedy, and soon they were cutting wires and other expensive materials and exchanging them at ridiculous prices. The garbage man now frequented the yard every day, and Tunde began to package the things for him beforehand, as long as payments met Tunde's needs for more food. Emeka had seen a few times when the things were exchanged, and had thought it was some set of unused items the same as he'd given the young man. He didn't know that money was being exchanged, and that even expensive wires were being cut and sold to the garbage guy.

However, as it was often said, ten days were for the thief, but one day for the house owner. Tunde was out of town, and the garbage man had come as usual to collect the items. He met another person, whom he didn't know was the supervisor. The supervisor had noticed the missing items and had been keeping records. He transferred Emeka to another unit and manned the gate. The garbage man had come, requesting to transact the way he often did. He asked about Tunde, and was informed Tunde wasn't available; he then inquired about Emeka. The supervisor played along, and asked what items were usually given to him and how much he paid for them. The garbage man stated all. He was told to wait while the items were brought. Meanwhile, the supervisor stepped out and notified the police. He requested a police officer to come by immediately. The items were neatly packaged as the garbage man had requested - wires, irons, bolts, etc. He made payment and loaded them on his truck. He thanked the supervisor and began to push his truck. But just then, two policemen in mufti who'd just arrived at the post apprehended the garbage man.

Emeka was summoned. He was asked if he had any dealing with the young man. He responded in affirmation, unaware that the man had been arrested. The garbage man had confessed to the supervisor and the police that he did the business with Tunde and Emeka, and that in fact Emeka was the first person to have offered the items to him.

The company quickly moved in to arrest Tunde, but discovered he'd moved out of his last known address. His surety had disappeared as well. The more Emeka insisted on his innocence, the less it was believed. The garbage man had maintained that Tunde informed him that he shared the proceeds with Emeka.

"And my good deeds caused this!" Emeka sighed loudly. Voices from the other inmates had stirred him back to reality. The general cell was already getting rowdy. Inmates walked up and down; some inmates would cross over others to get through. The food bell had just rung and someone had made a joke about beans, and the inmates laughed. It was in Hausa; Emeka didn't get it. He guessed it was something about the food, the beans, the watery beans.

**

The mental enslavement was more damaging than the physical confinement. Every inmate would have that experience, with not much difference. On the day of his admission, as the security van drove to the prison gate and stopped, Emeka and all other detainees were led out of the vehicle. The police prosecutor handed the warrants over to the prison officials who were waiting at the prison gate. The Prison Official in charge of gate duties took the warrants to ascertain that they had all the features of a valid warrant, then he called out the names on each warrant and as the detainee answered, he was uncuffed and led into the prison yard where an admission board was waiting.

The prison admission board, made up of the Superintendent in charge of the prison, an industry man, record officer, nurse, doctor, chief warden, and psychologist, would go on to search, examine, counsel, and classify the inmate before he was admitted. Items found on the inmate were held by the record officer.

Emeka wasn't really bothered; he had nothing of worth except his handset. And he was told he wouldn't need it. The prison provided a phone for calls.

"Emeka, live your life here as though this is your permanent home." The psychologist on the admission board had told him. "Some inmates come here believing they will leave the next day, and when it doesn't happen they get depressed and suicidal. Take one step at a time and you will be fine." He'd believed he was offering much needed counselling.

The rest of the admission board sounded identical and harsh. It presupposed the prison officials didn't want inmates nursing unrealistic hopes. But what hopes could such a person supposedly have?

The moment the big prison gate was bolted, Emeka's heart

rate quickened. The sound had made him turn to look at the giant gate. This minute, he realized that his freedom was gone. In the coming weeks, months, and perhaps years, he would be sharing space, food, and everything with thieves, armed robbers, and murderers. He couldn't withhold the tears that ran down his cheek. And when he turned, a guy beside him was crying.

The prison was a community of its own where you would find inmates called President, Governors, Ministers, Police, Lawyers, Judges, and all the other elements you find in the society. There were rules, and inmates kept to them.

A trial was ongoing the afternoon Emeka was admitted. The presiding judge had paused when the warder brought Emeka into the cell. And so had everyone else as they examined the new intake. An inmate received Emeka from the Chief Warder and took him to a corner.

"I am Adam. A trial is going on," he said. "Keep calm, let me show you your space."

Adam was in his early thirties. He was short, dark-skinned, with narrow shoulders. He looked like he may have once been muscular but had lost the muscle tone.

"What is the trial about?" Emeka asked, as he followed the inmate. The place was very quiet, with young, despondent faces everywhere he looked.

"Speak quietly before the court, or the judge will hold you in contempt," Adam cautioned Emeka. "That guy in a red top stole food the other man's wife brought to him. The court is deciding on it."

"Sit down here. This is your space." Adam showed Emeka and crawled back to his own space. Emeka got to know from another inmate, a twenty-one years old sitting next to him, that Adam was the Provost and it was his job to welcome new inmates. He would inform them of the rules and ways of the prison.

The judge, satisfied Emeka had settled, resumed the proceedings.

In the days that followed, Emeka learnt that the inmates settled issues by trials before presenting the same to the wardens. The parties in the suits were often represented by other inmates who acted as lawyers. The judge was a lawyer who was serving a life sentence for manslaughter. He was called the Chief Judge. He sat over cases of fighting, sodomy, stealing, and occasionally, attempted suicide. Violent inmates who tried to take the life of other inmates or theirs were kept in isolation cells. Emeka hoped and prayed such heinous acts wouldn't occur while he was there. The problem was that he wouldn't know how long he would be there.

It dawned on him that the hours had turned to days and soon maybe weeks. He just realized why he was told to jettison thoughts of leaving the next day. He'd begun to settle in and accept the fact that he might well spend months or years in prison. He hadn't had a visit from his lawyer and that was unlike him. Earlier in the day, he had told Adam that he would need to speak with his lawyer.

"Aren't you going to the welfare office to use the phone?" Adam asked. They had become best of friends over the past days.

"A wise farmer in my village, Mazi Chinedu, usually says, the reason he doesn't mention snakes in his yam farm is so the yam cords don't suddenly become one. There is power in our thoughts and words."

"You and your proverbs, Emeka!"

"What can I do? Proverbs are one of the legacies I cherish about my grandmother," Emeka responded excitedly. Indeed, he was right; a child who was raised by his grandmother in the village, if he wasn't expert on how to blow the fireplace with his mouth, he would be on how to apply proverbs.

Emeka was sitting on a bench under a tree in an open space watching as tailors and their apprentices practiced their craft. He'd ignored the crafts because he felt he wouldn't be there for long. He might as well reconsider, he thought.

"Take it easy with your thoughts, Emeka." Adam knew Emeka spent long minutes staring into space while his mind journeyed.

"But what do I do, Adam? I was supposed to be here for only a few days. My bail application was granted, it's just hard to meet the conditions." Emeka believed it was the only way he could dwell less in the present.

"That is why I'm letting you know that your case is different. Stop holding a grudge against your lawyer and call him. You never can tell what made it impossible for him to come here. Is he even all right?"

Adam was right. A man whose parents paid the bride price of his wife basks in the euphoria that marriage was cheap. Would he have been taking Mr Tim's benevolence for granted? He thought. God forbid! Mr Tim had been like an elder brother. He'd taken up the matter for a fee but when Emeka couldn't pay, he'd waived the costs and done the matter without charging any fee. Sometimes, he spent money to buy food and other things for Emeka. Something was wrong. In court on the first date, he had informed Emeka he would come to the prison but hadn't shown up. It'd been over a week. It was unlike him. Trying to avoid communication with him was rather an act of foolishness. Emeka got up and followed Adam to the welfare office.

CHAPTER 4

Pius beamed as he looked out of the window into the hazy skies of Abuja city. As the plane descended, the beautiful, rocky landscapes came to view. The setting sun turned the sky into orange-blue. The Arik plane touched down on the Abuja tarmac exactly at 5:00 p.m.

It had been an eventful flight. 76 minutes, from the Murtala Muhammed Airport, Lagos to the Nnamdi Azikiwe International Airport. The first-class cabin was cozy, as usual. Pius had spent most of the time on the smooth and turbulence-free flight chatting with a young lady seated beside him. Thara was a post-graduate student at Baze University, and he was touched by her sophistication. He was easily drawn to ladies who could engage knowledgeably in discussions. She wasn't outstandingly beautiful, but her brilliance made up for whatever was lacking. He liked his women that way. It made him reminisce about his years and his class of women. It reminded him of the many times he'd ended up in hotels with the ladies he'd met on planes. *It's been ages*, he thought. It had been ages since he'd flown at all. He collected her number with hopes they would find time to hang out at a later date.

Nick and his crew were waiting at the Arrivals section of

the domestic wing. Nick and Pius had spoken briefly before he boarded the flight, and Nick had told him Madam was waiting. Pius had spent a few bucks trying to look different. He hadn't quite come to terms with expending the wad of dollars he had been given. First off, he wasn't sure he would be given such money again by Madam, so he needed to be careful with how he spent it. The thought of such cash on him made him feel rich. Secondly, even if he were to buy clothes, he was convinced he could find genuine articles in Abuja. Oddly, Lagos had more places to shop in, but one had to be careful not to buy fake items. Pius loathed wearing imitation designer clothes. He also wanted to have the money for security should the deal turn sour. He knew he had a weakness for money and would have to control it before it got him into further trouble, like it had years ago.

"Where is your car parked?" Pius asked.

Nick led the way, accompanied by two other muscled hands. One would easily take them for security guards.

"At the VIP car park. And your luggage?" Nick asked. He had expected another bag aside from the hand luggage.

"That's all." Pius stated. They walked out of the airport. Pius looked up, taking in his surroundings, and inhaled deeply. He smiled to himself rather oddly.

"It's good to be home."

He walked swiftly. The guards were swift as well, leaving Nick dragging himself behind. The band quickly made its way to two SUVs.

"The Range or the G-Wagon, sir?" one of the guards asked.

"The G-Wagon would be fine." Pius responded and as the guard opened the door, he immediately jumped into the back seat and stretched himself.

"Welcome, sir, I hope you enjoyed your flight?" The driver

grinned and crooked his head over his shoulder. Pius simply nodded and closed his eyes.

Nick finally caught up with the Range Rover and took his time to tuck himself completely into the back seat. But once he did, the guard closed the door, the cars drove off.

* * *

Aside from the condolence register, with a framed image of Chief next to it, nothing looked different. One could have thought the man was away on a short trip.

Pius stopped at the entrance and turned towards the register. He looked at the picture. The billionaire was smiling.

"So, you are dead, Chief," he muttered to himself, looking over the compound littered with several cars – a Range Rover, Bentley, another G-wagon, and Toyota Land Cruiser Jeep. Goose pimples sprang up all over his skin. Memories of his moments spent with Chief flashed through his mind, how they met, though accidental, and how he'd been his lawyer over the years.

He picked up the golden pen, struggling with shaky hands to scribble a condolence message. He was the fourth person on the register.

He dropped the pen and followed Nick, who used his thick body to push open the door leading into the mansion.

They stepped into the sitting room and met Madam Jennifer laughing. Catching sight of them, she paused and quickly stood up.

"You are welcome, Barrister Pius," she said and threw a stern look at Nick, dismissing him.

Nick hovered like a confused pet momentarily unsure of its owner's instructions before he disappeared into the lobby.

There was a young man sitting next to Madam Jennifer. He'd

been staring at Pius as soon as he walked in, eagle-eyed. Pius tried not to pay any attention to him, but he failed with each attempt. The young man was well dressed. Perfectly made hair, bearded, with toned skin. Gigolo was written all over him, and if one thought hard, the conclusion reached would be that he truly had nothing more to offer than his looks. And older yet unmarried women and divorcees would do anything to keep men with those looks to themselves.

"Excuse us," Madam Jennifer finally uttered to the young man, in a pleading tone. She would have avoided making the request, but she noticed the unspoken exchanges between the two men.

The young man reluctantly stood up. Madam smiled at him, urging him to retreat into the mansion.

"Gozy, I will be with you shortly," she said as he left.

"Please sit down," she said to Pius, trying her best to look like someone mourning her husband.

CHAPTER 5

Tim sat on the second row in the courtroom. Over the past few days, a lot had changed; only a tiny ray of light shone through the gloomy events that had taken place, one of which was his perfection of Emeka's bail and the latter's release from prison. Chris had assisted with that. Emeka had been very happy when he finally left the prison, and since they arrived at the court, he had been reluctant to leave Tim's side. He was with him until there were several lawyers in court. Suddenly, there were many lawyers looking for places to sit. Tim asked Emeka to take a seat at the back of the courtroom.

"Lawyers can't stand in court while parties are seated. They have first right of seating," he explained.

Emeka left to find a seat. Tim began to examine the documents in his file, what he had been able to gather so far. Most of the material for the case was in his stolen vehicle.

"Excuse me, Counsel," a lawyer stated as he attempted to squeeze himself into the space beside Tim. Tim adjusted and continued what he was doing.

He looked around to check if the other parties in the case were also in court. He saw the Prosecutor sitting on the opposite end of the courtroom, and wondered how he hadn't noticed

when the confrontational man walked in. He couldn't see anyone representing the nominal complainant, the company, except
they sent someone different from the person he saw in court on
the last adjourned date. Counsel to the first defendant was sitting
on the second row behind the Prosecutor.

Tim was still looking over his shoulder, trying to figure out
who else was in court for the matter. He exchanged nods and
smiles with other lawyers.

Then there were three bangs on the door leading into the
judge's chamber.

"Coooooooourt!" The clerk shouted. Everyone stood.

The Magistrate walked in and bowed; everyone in the court
followed suit.

"Good morning, everyone," she said. "This morning, the
court is full because we have a lot of cases. We will take the
criminal matters first and then the Registrar can call those matters not going on so we can decongest the court," she continued,
examining the full courtroom.

"Registrar, call the first criminal matter on the cause list."

"Case Number One on the cause list, criminal case for hearing between Commissioner of Police and Adamu Iro." The registrar handed the case file to the Magistrate.

Emeka quickly rushed to Tim.

"Sir, is that our case?"

"No, it isn't. Go back to where you were sitting. You don't run
around in court and let the magistrate see you. You will hear your
name when our case is called." Emeka returned to his seat.

"Are the parties in court?" the Magistrate asked and studied
the courtroom before writing in her record book.

"Appearances?"

"With utmost humility to this Honourable Court, I am A.
Abubakar for the Prosecution." Mr Abubakar was one of the

privileged police officers that had studied law while in practice. He'd joined the force as a corporal, rising to the rank of inspector before he was called to the Nigerian bar and with the passage of the Administration of Criminal Justice Act which abolished the prosecution of cases by ranking police officers, he quickly switched over to be a lawyer, taking up cases in various magistrate courts and had gained recognition over the years.

"Defence?"

"No legal representation, Your Worship. Your Worship will recall that on the last adjourned date, the defendants and their counsel also didn't make it to court."

"Is that so, and they were aware of the date?" the magistrate asked as she flipped through her record book.

"Yes, Your Worship. They deliberately did not make court today. There is no excuse for that."

"Are the defendants on bail?"

"Yes, Your Worship, and we shall be applying for the revocation of their bail."

"Go ahead and make your application, Prosecution."

"As the court pleases. Your Worship, we apply for the first and second defendants' bail to be revoked. The defendants are unwilling to stand trial before this court and have absconded. We have made efforts to reach their surety to no avail."

"Application for the revocation of the bail of the first and second defendants is hereby granted. Warrants of arrest are to be issued against the first and second defendants. This case is adjourned to the twenty-third of June for continuation of trial."

"Thank you, Your Worship, may I seek the indulgence of this court to call Case Number Three on the cause list, out of turn. I'm also in that matter."

"Okay, Mr Abubakar. Registrar, kindly call Case Number Three."

"The next case is a criminal case for hearing, between Commissioner of Police and Yunus Gaddo, Tunde Edun, and Emeka Okoromadu."

"Are the defendants in court?" the Magistrate inquired.

Emeka was already standing in the dock. He had rushed into the dock the moment he heard his name. He was infuriated by the sight of the garbage man, Yunus Gaddo, whom he hadn't seen since the last adjourned date. Their eyes met and he felt anger rise within him.

"Your Worship, the first and third defendants are in court. The second defendant is at large, and we are still making efforts to arrest him."

"Okay, the situation is noted. Have the defendants taken their plea?"

"Yes, Your Worship."

"Legal representation?"

"With utmost humility to this Honourable Court, I am A. Abubakar Esq, for the Prosecution."

"May it please Your Worship, Bulus N. Bulus Esq, for the Second Defendant, Your Worship."

"Tim Akpan Esq. My humble appearance is for the Third Defendant. My Lord, I have an application before this Honourable Court."

"Mr Akpan, we will get to that. Prosecution, what is the business of the day?"

"Your Worship, the matter is slated for trial; we plan to call our first witness, PW1."

"Mr Akpan, what is your application?" the Magistrate inquired.

"Your Worship, we shall be asking for time to prepare for the trial. I was robbed of my car and the proof of evidence and other documents prepared for this case were in the vehicle. It has destabilized me and I'm currently applying for certified true copies of those I can obtain. Therefore, I shall be asking for a date, Your Worship."

"I'm sorry about that, Mr Akpan. Prosecution, any objection to the application for adjournment?"

"Your Worship, we sympathize with the defence counsel. While we will not object to his application for an adjournment, we wish it to be on the record that the adjournment is at the instance of the Defendant."

"Mr Abubakar, Mr Akpan said he was robbed of his car and you can be sorry for him, we should take his word for it."

"Your Worship, there is nothing before this court to establish what counsel is saying. No evidence or document is before this court to prove that his car was stolen as alleged."

"Your Worship, I take exception to this. Does this mean I will be willing to lie to the court?"

"That's enough, counsel. What we shall do is to take the evidence of the Prosecution's first witness while other witnesses will be taken on another date. Call your witness, Mr Abubakar."

"Your Worship, the fact is that our witness isn't in court today as he had a family emergency. His wife sustained burns from hot water while cooking this morning."

"So, you are not even ready, Mr Abubakar, and you acted as though your witness was in court. Please don't do that next time."

"As the court pleases." The litigants as well as their counsel in court chorused and there was a chorus of noise as people talked about Mr Abubakar and his insistence even when he wasn't ready. It took the caution of the Magistrate before the courtroom became quiet again.

"Mr Akpan, how long do you need to get your house in order? Take note that this is a criminal matter and the trial must be given accelerated hearing."

"Your Worship, two or three weeks is sufficient for me. I will have filed and regularized all my processes before then."

At this point, the Registrar quickly called out some dates available in the court's diary.

"Is that convenient to all parties?"

"Yes, Your Worship!" All the counsel on the matter chorused.

"This matter is adjourned to the twentieth of July for hearing."

"Thank you, Your Worship."

Tim bowed and hurriedly left the court. Emeka quickly bowed and ran towards Tim, escaping an unpleasant moment with Yunus.

CHAPTER 6

Rita opened her eyes at about 5:00 a.m. She really couldn't tell why she was awake one hour before her alarm was scheduled to go off. On the other hand, she was glad she didn't have to be woken up by the cranky sound. She despised the sound even though she couldn't do without it. With the cold weather, it was the only way she could get ready on time and not miss the train to work.

She lay on her back with her duvet stretched up to her face. The heater in her condo fought to beat the cold. That morning, the temperature was below zero degrees in East London.

She stared blankly at the ceiling of her condo—white, plain ceiling, heater vent, dim lights illuminating only the ceiling area. She hadn't been sleeping much lately and hadn't found last night's sleep refreshing either.

She continued to stare at the ceiling without thoughts or ideas and was still sleepy-eyed. She would have to get up by 6:00 a.m. to get ready, and she just might catch some sleep for another hour. She sort of assumed that wasn't likely though.

She rolled over till her feet touched the ground and she grabbed the sheets and wrapped them around her body. She sidestepped haggardly towards the wall till her hand reached the light switch. She flicked on the switch.

Her condo was a studio apartment. From where she stood, she could see dirty plates in the kitchen sink. And then the pile of dirty clothes. She hated the fact she would have to do the chores by herself, one of the reasons she despised London. Abroad you had to do everything by yourself, it wasn't like that in Nigeria.

Rita ignored the chores and went to her fridge. She took a glass and an unfinished bottle of vodka and went straight to the fluffy rug beside her bed.

This wouldn't be complete without shisha, she thought.

She dropped the vodka and glass and went to pick her hookah. It would take her a few minutes to set it up, add the charcoal, and get it ready, but she didn't mind as long as it satisfied her craving for Tobacco. The next twenty minutes saw Rita seated on the floor, sipping her drink, sucking and puffing smoke into the air. Soon, her room was hazy and warmer.

At 6:00 a.m., there was a knock on her door. She ignored it. Another rattle on the door, more loudly this time.

"Who the fuck!" Rita exclaimed as she dropped the pipe, got up, and staggered to the door. She held in to her glass of vodka.

"Who the hell is that?" she screamed. She'd been smoking for thirty minutes; a few minutes more and she would cross the 100-cigarettes mark.

"It's Willow!"

Willow was her British workmate, twenty-three years old but shy and submissive. They had been friends since the day Willow was attacked on her way from work. Before then, she'd ignored Rita, considering her a "nasty African". Two boys had attacked her on her way from work and were about to hurt her. Rita had charged at them with all the nerve she could muster and hit them with sticks, stones, planks, and everything she could lay her hands on. The boys had been startled at her tenacity and had let go of Willow. She grabbed Willow and they ran. That night, Willow slept at her place and since then, they were best of friends. They soon found out they didn't live far from each other.

"Rita, it's smoky in here." Willow stated as she struggled through the smoke-filled room.

"Yeah. You wanna have some?" Rita asked.

"Nay, I'm going to work. Aren't you ready for work? It's six o'clock, the train leaves in ten minutes."

"I'm not going." Rita forced a reply.

"Why not? You just got back from your leave, you can't stay away from work just like that," Willow stated, a note of fear and warning in her tone.

Rita looked at her, uncertain whether her worries were borne out of concern for her or for the protection she felt around her. Willow always said Rita behaved like a man. To that, Rita would always smile and tell her it was because she was trained like a boy, by her father who wanted a boy so much and since her mother died, her stepmother hadn't been good to her either. Willow had this cloud of protection anytime she was with Rita. She wouldn't want to trade it for anything. She would lose that if Rita lost her job.

"I'm not going. I lost my father and I will have to travel back to Nigeria."

"Oh, I'm so sorry, Rita. I didn't know that and you just got back from Nigeria a while ago," Willow said and hugged Rita. She wasn't certain of the right manner to console her African friend. She wished there was more she could do.

"I will be fine." Rita backed away from Willow. She didn't look bereaved as Willow had seen other Africans that lost loved ones and if not for her mentioning it, one wouldn't think she was grieving. *Maybe aside being hysteric, this was another way Africans*

grieved she didn't know about; maybe that was why she woke up
smoking and drinking, to fight off the thoughts, Willow thought,
but then Rita drank and smoked anytime, practically doing any-
thing she wanted to do.

"You can leave now so you don't miss the train," Rita stated
after a moment of silence. She wanted her friend out so she could
finish up her booze and get set for her day. Even though she
wouldn't be going to work, she knew she would have a busy day.

"Okay. I will check on you when I'm back," Willow said as
she waved at Rita and made for the door.

"We will see then. Let's go clubbing tonight."

"Anything you say." Willow left the apartment.

Rita locked the door and went back to the rug where she had
left the shisha.

For the next hour Rita smoked, drank and thought about her
life. She would have to plan the strategy for the World War III
about to go down in Nigeria. She would have to take care of a
lot of things and make sure her stepmother, "that witch", didn't
outsmart her.

Again, she was intensely irritated at the thought of the fact
that her father was worth billions while she served pizza to customers in a restaurant in London.

"Daddy, I would like to work in one of your companies,"
she'd begged him on her graduation. He'd promised to look into
it but that was where it ended. When she'd pressured him more,
he had said that he would need her to change before he gave her
any such opportunity.

"You are too damn wild, Rita," he said.

"Too damned wild and you let your daughter go through pain
every day. Wake up at 6 a.m., bathe with cold water, wear many
clothes, and rush to meet up with the train so I could go serve

people pizza in some god-forsaken restaurant. What billionaire does that?" Rita questioned him.

"That's my principle! You set yours when you make your money. It's my billions, my rules. I've done everything a father could do for his beloved child. Good education, good health care, money to take care of basic needs, but as you stepped out of reach, you decided to go wild," he would always say.

Rita knew most of what he said was true, if not all, but most of it. She just couldn't get herself to agree. Her pride wouldn't let her.

Suddenly, something crossed her mind. Did her father leave a will? She hadn't thought of this all along. Her little knowledge of the law could be so inimical. She wondered why she was only thinking of this now and not before, not when she was in Nigeria.

"Shit!" She got angrier. The thought of him making a will scared her even more. Would he add her to the will? How are wills made? Was she even entitled to inherit his property as a female? What could she do to change this? So many thoughts sprang into her head at once.

She knew she had to head back to Nigeria. She would scramble for any of the properties he had in London, see which she could get hold of before leaving for the inevitable war in Nigeria.

She looked around at the condo. He'd bought the place for her to live in when she gained admission. She was his little princess then. She could start with the condo. She had the documents, she thought.

Undoubtedly, she was troubled with thoughts of many things she needed to put in place before leaving London. She gulped the rest of the vodka, unzipped and undid her nightgown and undies, letting them drop on the floor.

She turned on the heater and stepped into the shower.

The time was now 7:43 a.m.

***

Tim arrived at the office by 10 a.m. He'd alternated between two magistrate courts, neither of which sat. He later learned from a court clerk that the Senior Magistrates in the Magisterial District were on a training break. He'd taken new dates off record; the matters were for his Head of Chamber and he was just tired of running up and down for the man and other seniors. He went back to the office to inform him of the new date.

"Why are you coming in at this time?" Patrick asked as he ran into Tim coming up the stairs to the office. Patrick was his immediate senior.

"Good morning, Barrister Patrick. I went to court." Tim made sure he added the "Barrister". Patrick was one of those lawyers who could strangle anyone who failed to address them as "barrister".

"Which court? Is that an office matter?" Patrick asked scornfully.

"Magistrate court." Tim noticed himself feeling utterly help-less, wishing Patrick would just step away and let him be.

But then that was just what Patrick wanted to hear, because senior advocates wouldn't take up matters in inferior courts. Patrick had asked so he could lampoon Tim. He found it fulfill-ing being condescending to junior lawyers.

"You spend hours running up and down doing your personal briefs. How do you think salaries are paid here?"

"What do you mean?" Tim asked. He was getting irritable and disgusted. He was about to lose it. One thing Patrick didn't know about Tim was his hot temper. He could be as irate as he was tolerant. In fact, because he was humble, he tolerated a lot of unpalatable behaviour, but when he snapped, it was as though the world would end right then.

Patrick was about to see that happen.

"Why must you go about doing personal cases when matters in the office are unfinished? What sort of rubbish is that?"

"I don't get you, Mr Patrick?" Tim silently wished the idiot wouldn't push him any further. He was drained, jumping from one court to another on public transport. Since he'd lost his car, moving around had been increasingly onerous.

"Have you followed up on Omah Lawal vs Inflow industries Ltd? The case that was struck out. Has it been relisted?"

"I have filed a motion for relisting; as I informed you, the bailiff wasn't able to serve the motion and the hearing notice on the other party to the suit."

"And you think that gives you the right to be doing personal briefs without the knowledge of the Learned Silk?" Patrick rudely interjected.

"Hey, Patrick or whatever you call yourself." Tim shouted as he dropped the file in his hand on the staircase.

"What?" Patrick screamed, unsure of what he'd just heard.

"Yes, Patrick. I'm sick and tired of your unbearable bossing around. I've had a terrible day on these matters for Mr Sam and you are the worst kind of pain I need to be piled on me right now."

Patrick angrily charged at Tim, for whatever he had in mind, perhaps to hold him, look him in the eyes, and warn him never to talk to him like that. But this didn't end well. Tim pushed him and he hit the edge of the staircase rail. He fell.

He tried getting up, but then missed his step. He was both awed and shaken. Of a truth, he wasn't a match for Tim in size and it seemed he just realized it. He often forgot he had a small build, or perhaps he knew this. That was why he would try to display his dominance at every opportunity.

Some colleagues had run down towards the ensuing pandemonium on the stairs. Ngozi, Tim's seat mate, was amongst the first to get there and she was the colleague he usually confided in. Tim was still charged up, fuming and stammering.

Patrick stood up, dusted himself off, stating that he would deal with Tim.

By then, the entire stairs were filled with lawyers and supporting staff of the office. The head of chambers had also come down.

There was a division amongst the lawyers, with junior lawyers going towards Tim. They surrounded him like someone who'd just won a trophy. No one had ever addressed Patrick in such a manner. The disappointing thing was that Patrick and a few other seniors had created so much bitterness and resentment within the office. The beautiful office set up by the Learned Silk had turned into a sad place with unhappy people who were there only because they didn't have many options. The Learned Silk didn't know this. The seniors didn't tell him and none of the juniors was bold enough to do so.

"Tim, you have no right to confront your senior," the head of chambers stated, after listening to Patrick. He didn't bother to hear what Tim had to say. The truth is that the bar was heavily anchored on seniority, not as to age but as to year of call to bar. But as they say, an elder who elects to play hide and seek games with children should not be seen complaining when pebbles are thrown at him. A senior at the bar who enjoys such privileges must not be seen superfluously abusing same.

"Seriously, Mr Sam?" Tim asked, puzzled at what had just happened. The juniors were angry and bickering as Patrick grumbled. His ego had just been pricked.

"It's so unfortunate," Tim started. "The Learned Silk wouldn't know what you guys have turned his office into. I wish he was in town to see this."

"Shut up!" Patrick shouted.

"I guess I'm done," Tim stated as he ran up towards his workspace.

Ngozi followed him.

"Tim, what are you doing?" Ngozi asked as she noticed Tim packing his things.

"I'm leaving. I can't take this shit anymore. I spent over N3,000 on taxis this morning running around for those idiots today only for me to get this? Ngozi, how much is our salary? And you are expected to kill yourself for that amount. The Learned Senior Advocate knows that amount can't take one anywhere. That was why he told us that his firm was a base for us to find our footing. Patrick and the rest wish to frustrate us all. I'm leaving."

"Don't go, Tim. Even if you are to leave, you have to resign properly and see the Learned Silk." She was right, it wasn't appropriate for Tim to leave without proper resignation being tendered and it was even more inappropriate, as Tim wasn't Patrick's employee nor any of the seniors. A handful of the juniors, about seven of them, had gathered, pleading with Tim to remain and report the matter to the Learned Silk upon his return.

Tim gave some thought to this, but his reality was that he was truly fed up. Over the past days, particularly since he'd lost his vehicle, he'd thought of leaving the firm but didn't have the courage to do so without tendering a resignation letter and meeting with the Learned Silk. He didn't wish it would be this dramatic, but he knew it was now time.

He needed time to focus on this new case he was handling for Emeka and some other matters whose case files were in the stolen vehicle. He wouldn't achieve that by running around for seniors and getting bashed by them at the same time. This had almost cost him Emeka's case when he couldn't find time to visit the young man in prison as he'd promised.

"I'm done!" he exclaimed.

The juniors, too, thought about the issue. One of them asked, "Seriously, Ngozi, why does he stay away from you?"

"Because he'd toasted me and I refused. But before I declined, I led him on, and he sent me some WhatsApp messages which he deleted but I had taken screenshots of them before he could delete them. The messages would certainly leave a dent on his ego if made public, which was why I sent them back to him so he would be aware I have them. He came to tell me that I shouldn't have taken screenshots of the messages, knowing that someone could see them. I didn't respond. He knows I still have the messages, so he hasn't caused me any trouble since then," Ngozi said, and they all laughed.

"Don't mind his drunken soul," another disgruntled lawyer commented.

By then, Tim was done packing and arranging his things. He'd called an Uber that was waiting for him downstairs. Ngozi and two juniors helped him take his things down to the car.

The car was just leaving the compound when the office secretary ran to inform Tim that the head of chambers was calling him.

"Calling me to do what? Please tell him his files are on his table." Tim turned to his driver, "Please start the trip."

CHAPTER 7

"Put in the *round-about*, not that one, the other one, yes, that and add the assorted over there." Pius looked into the pot full of meat before him.

"*Oga, make I add this liver?*" The girl serving asked and tossed the meat with her long spoon.

"Yes, add that. Add the 'towel' also." Pius stated. "Also, add that beef I'm seeing there." He pointed at another big pot.

"This one?" She stirred the content of the pot with her spoon and scooped a chunk of meat out.

"Yes, that one."

"*Oga*, may I put in *amala* or *semo*?"

"*Amala*, of course."

The serving girl was dressed in a T-shirt bearing "Amala Place" on it and an apron hanging over her neck. She quickly put everything together and poured *gbegiri* on the food. She moved to the cashier and gestured towards Pius to follow and make payment. Done with him, she moved to the next customer in line. The girls were all trying to beat the growing line of customers.

"How much is yours?" Pius asked as he joined Thara who was already at the cashier.

"The cashier said N3,650 for everything," Thara said as she turned to look at Pius. "You sure you want to pay?" She tried to find her debit card in her purse.

"I got this." Pius said and stepped forward to the cashier. He pulled out some N1000 notes and handed them to the cashier.

"I'm paying for hers and mine." He said as he pointed to his tray of food that had been kept beside the cashier.

"This place is really nice," Pius said as he looked around. "Amala Place" was inscribed on every available surface. A soft afrobeat, "Ye" by Burna Boy, played in the background.

Pius was momentarily lost in thought as he surveyed the environment. Lots of people, smartly dressed, apparently working class, rushed in while the girls struggled to keep up with their orders. The place was neat, with nice tables, plastic chairs, and African set fittings.

The cashier confirmed the money, issued him a receipt with his balance, and turned to the next customer. Pius and Thara picked up their trays and walked to an empty table.

"Amala Place. Amala Place in Abuja!" Pius said feeling really impressed.

"I said you would like it." Thara smiled. She sat facing Pius. They washed their hands, impatient to devour the meal.

As Pius washed his hands, he stared at Thara. She was elegant and the neatly styled *kente* fabric she wore made her look even classier. He'd wondered when last he had a moment with such a classy woman. They had run into each other on the plane, reluctantly exchanged numbers, thinking she was in a relationship and may not have time for him. He'd messaged just for the sake of doing something. She'd replied an hour after and since then they'd chatted for long intervals on WhatsApp and not long after, they were spending hours over the phone.

She had been at his hotel for two nights and where they had fun. But not as rough as he would have liked.

To make up, Nick had hooked him up with some ladies, but they had been what they were, to pass the time, nothing more. He liked to try new things. For some reason, he noticed he hadn't completely lost his wings. He hadn't lost his wooing skills either. He'd been wrong to think he had.

He noticed that he was fast becoming used to Thara and lately, they hung out a lot. He knew he liked her. She was smart, ambitious, and classy, the way he liked his women, except for something he wasn't too sure about. She wasn't crazy enough the way he loved his girls.

Thara had kept to her word to show him round Abuja. He'd been in the UK, he lied, and hadn't visited town for a while. She promised to take him to see the city and they had visited some places, had dinner, lunch, and even bowled at Domes. Indeed, Abuja had changed a lot within a span of three years, he thought.

Pius had been hanging out a lot with Thara, so much that he forgot he had old enemies in town. His behaviour could be likened to a hen that roamed about with its chick in the open to convince the cock it wasn't barren, forgetting that there were hawks in the sky. He was supposed to stay low.

Over the past few days, he'd spent more time with women than with any other thing. If he wasn't with the ladies, he was with Madam. Of course, she too was a woman, a different kind of woman though, not his type. The time he'd spent with Madam, they had gone through the properties taking note of the will. She had shown it to him, in an envelope, and they'd agreed to only open it when the entire family was around. That would be Chief's wish and it was the appropriate thing to do.

He had also made his enquiries at the probate office in Abuja, and he was reliably informed that Chief had lodged a will. She was right after all; if so, there was nothing to worry about. The FCT High Court, Abuja, Probate Office wasn't a place you could play pranks.

"Are you enjoying the meal?" Thara asked.

"Enjoying is like saying—"

"Excuse me, you look like someone I know," a voice said in Pius's ear.

He instinctively turned.

"Payilo?" The man screamed. "I said it. I was certain you were the one!"

Pius hadn't heard that name in more than three years. He froze, unsure of what to say or do. He could deny he was the one and claim the young man was mistaken; the man wasn't someone you could do that with. Not Baro.

"Baro, what are you doing here?" Pius asked

"I should be asking you that," Baro stated as he hugged Pius. He was so elated. "That's my wife." He beckoned a lady tagging along but not saying anything.

"Good evening, sir." The woman greeted him and bent her knees.

"That's Madam?" Baro asked, glancing between Pius and the lady to see who would confirm his guess.

"That's my very good friend, Thara,"

"Wow! So good to see you. Everyone thought you were dead!" Baro said. "We should keep in touch. Please type your phone number and I will call you." He handed over his phone.

Pius took the phone and inputted some numbers, an old line he wasn't using anymore.

"I will call. I will call," Baro said and walked to his wife who'd stepped aside, waiting for him to finish. They waved and left. They had bought their food dished in *takeaway*.

"Amazing! That's your name? Payilo. It's so cute." Thara turned to Pius.

"Please don't call me that," Pius said.

"But it's cute. I like it. What does it mean?"

"I actually don't like it." Pius tried to sound as cool as he could. "I wouldn't want to be called that. I think we need to leave." He was suddenly aware of the dangers he may have put himself in. News would spread that he was alive and was in fact, in town. It was so reckless of him.

Thara quietly obliged. She cleaned up, got up, and they left the restaurant.

CHAPTER 8

"Metro Plaza. *Abeg,* do you know where Metro Plaza is?" Emeka inquired from a girl setting her things down to roast plantain.

"It's ahead, three plazas away." She pointed and moved away.

Emeka thanked her and continued down the street.

MB Plaza. No, not it. Okon Mall. Abura Plaza. He counted. The girl said three plazas away, he'd counted four plazas and hadn't seen it yet. Looking ahead he saw the "Metr Plaza". The "o" on the nameplate had fallen off, and it now read "Metr".

Emeka strolled into the compound.

"I'm looking for the law firm of Barrister Tim," he said to a group of young men, chatting in front of one of the shops.

"Is there a law firm here?" One of the men asked.

"I don't think there is a lawyer's office here," the rest affirmed.

"Suit B16, Metro Plaza." Emeka brought out the piece of paper where he had written the address.

"Oh, that's at the back. I think it's a security firm or something. Take the stairs, on the second floor, turn left. The office is there."

Emeka thanked them and moved on.

He met a security guard at the lobby who directed him to take the stairs, the lift wasn't working.

"B16! That's it!" he said quietly to himself the moment the office tag matched the number on his paper.

Tim and Chris were in the office discussing matters before Emeka arrived. Tim had been in since 8:00 a.m. While he'd been early because there was much more they had to discuss, it was also because he had no office. He'd told Chris he resigned, and Chris offered him one of the rooms in his office.

"You can use this anytime," he said.

That had been a great relief. Tim would get most of his law books and set a table and chair in the place for client meetings. One thing that gladdened him the most was, this time, he wouldn't have to hide his case files from anyone.

"Emeka, come in," Tim called out from his inner office.

The receptionist led Emeka through the glass barrier to the office where Tim and Chris were seated.

"Welcome, Emeka." Tim beckoned him to sit down.

"Good afternoon, Mr Tim, good afternoon, sir," Emeka greeted both men.

"This is my new office. I hope you didn't have any difficulty locating it?" Tim asked, to which Emeka shook his head.

"Do you care for something to drink?" Chris had opened a desk fridge beside him and brought out a bottle of malt. He offered it to Emeka, who gladly took it and opened it immediately. He hadn't eaten since morning and had walked a long distance to get to the place.

"Thank you, sir." Emeka stated, obviously relieved after the first gulp.

A moment of silence followed. Both men noticed the young man was hungry and so they let him finish his drink. He dropped the empty can in the waste bin and sat down.

"We have news for you." Tim broke the silence.

"Bad news?" Emeka's heart skipped, afraid that something was amiss about the news. The village town crier cries loudest when it is bad news. He quickly flashed back to the prison, and he couldn't bear anything that would return him to prison.

"Good news. Good news, really." Tim smiled, unsure of how to go about the entire news. "I know you can't wait to hear it. Let me tell you now, the case against you has been dropped."

"Dropped?" Emeka jumped up and ran towards Tim. He hugged him so tightly and wouldn't let go.

"Emeka, let go. Let go! It's not just me you should be thanking, you should thank Mr Chris here. He did most of the work." Tim forcefully released himself from Emeka's grip.

"Thank you, Sir. Thank you, Sir!" Emeka knelt before Chris. He knew he couldn't hug him, but he was overwhelmed with joy.

"The prosecution decided to drop the charges against you because we found Tunde," Chris happily stated.

"God, you know I am innocent! Ibu Chukwu Emeka. The same God that could part the Red Sea. Chukwu Okike who could fetch water with a basket, the same God who could crack the coconut with an egg. Nothing is beyond you!" He screamed, stretching his hands before heavens, still on his knees. He was crying.

"The police will cut a deal. If you collaborate with them to prosecute Tunde. They need you as their witness and—"

"Anything. I can do anything." Emeka got up and wiped his eyes.

"We have more news for you. We don't know how to go about this one," Tim said.

"Where is your mother?" Chris asked Emeka.

"My mom?" Emeka responded, wondering why he was being asked that.

"My... my mom is dead," he stuttered, wondering why the question. If they didn't have bad news, why would they be asking him about his mother?

"What about your father? Wait. You mean the woman who gave birth to you is dead?" Chris asked as he fixed his eyes directly on Emeka, who was suddenly nauseated and uncomfortable.

"I never knew who my father was. I never met him. I was raised by my grandmother, who is dead, and she's the one I called Mom," he said, wishing Chris would stop the questioning. "What is going on, Mr Tim?"

"Actually, we want to know about your real mother. We have something we have to tell you about your father."

"My mother isn't someone I like to talk about. I don't know where she is now and I don't care to know. We don't talk. She abandoned me when I was just a little child. I think she's in Europe or something. She is wicked and callous."

"Don't talk about your mother like that. She's still your mother." It was Chris this time, and he knew he was beginning to sound like the bad cop. But someone had got to tell the boy the truth.

"We have found your father," Tim said.

"What are you saying, please? My father from where?"

"Chief Peter Onu. The Chief Executive Officer of the engineering company you work, or used to work, for is your father."

"What sort of news is this, Barrister?" Emeka struggled to suppress his anger.

Tim urged Chris to go ahead and tell him everything. Chris took his time to narrate to Emeka how a woman had tried to blackmail Chief Onu using the knowledge of a son he didn't know he had and how Chief had hired him to investigate the matter, how he had obtained Emeka's hair strand and conducted a DNA test proving that Chief was his father. It was a hard knock but for some reason, Emeka began to believe the whole thing. Whether he did so because the person being talked about was the multibillionaire oil mogul or not, was another thing altogether.

"Are you saying that after so many years, suddenly I have a father, and perhaps a sister, and a stepmother?" Emeka was sarcastic.

"We don't want to bank on that yet. They won't receive you, just be certain of that," Tim added.

"We have a problem," Chris stated.

"Problem! As if I knew it. The pains that turn into whitlow start as a prickle. You can't come up with such news without a problem." He'd been expecting them to say something bad.

"The problem is we can't really make headway with the family without your mother," Chris went on.

"Then I'm not interested," Emeka retorted and stood up. He would rather leave than hear more about this nonsense. They had done enough getting him out of the police mess. Aside from that, the rest of what they were saying wasn't making any sense.

"Sit down, Emeka," Tim said irritably. "What is wrong with you? We are telling you that we just discovered you are heir to Chief Onu's wealth and you are here making a fuss. Do you know how much that will come to? If you don't want the money, *we* need it. You know how much effort and resources I've spent trying to get you out of prison? Suddenly God has given us a breakthrough and you are here acting abysmally."

"Tell him, and in fact, we need to discuss with him how much in percentage he's paying us for all this. I don't understand this boy."

"I will draw up terms that he will sign."

"I'm sorry," Emeka apologised as he recalled the words of his grandmother that the lizard says it is so much better to avoid quarrels that it nods in agreement even before the question is asked. "I'm not ungrateful for all you have done for me. The only thing is that I haven't had a good time with my mother and I don't want anything to do with her for now."

"Don't worry, leave it to us to handle her. Do you know how we can reach her?"

"You shouldn't condemn her. She was the one who reached out to Chief to tell him about you. She doesn't know where you are and I'm sure she will be looking for you," Chris added.

"I can't contact her, but I can find someone who has her number or a way to reach her. I think she speaks with my Uncle, my grandma's younger brother. I will speak with him to get his number. He is in the village."

"Okay then. Do that and get back to us. We need her. We don't know how Chief's family will react to this. We need her to establish that truly Chief was your father. Chief knew about you before he died, and he'd planned to introduce you to his family. I was looking for you, not knowing you were in prison. We aren't giving up on this," Tim stated.

"I will try."

Chris opened his drawer and brought out some money which he handed over to Emeka.

"Go and eat and take this for your transport back home. Be careful."

Emeka thanked them and left the office.

CHAPTER 9

At noon, Pius called the hotel reception requesting lunch to be served in his room. Not long after he dropped the intercom, Room Service knocked to bring the tray of food exquisitely served the Burney Hotel way. He ate, drank out of the bottle of Chandon wine, and was wondering what next to do with himself. He wasn't going anywhere, he concluded. Unless Madam called, nothing else mattered other than to rest. It was the only reasonable thing to do. Thara had called to say that she would be traveling to Taraba. It was some family emergency and she would say more when next they spoke. She would be away for a week, she had said.

He would shower and take a nap afterwards, he thought. He walked over to the wardrobe to pick something to change into once he came out of the shower. He was just about to drop the clothes and step into the shower when he heard the rattle on the door.

Room Service again, he thought. He put on his boxers and singlet and went to open the door.

"Good afternoon," a tall, young lady said, grinning from ear to ear.

"You aren't Room Service. You don't look like them, so who are you?"

The lady smiled, bowing her head to pass through the space beneath Pius's hand which he held against the door frame, and walked into the room. He made to shout at her but couldn't tell why he found it difficult to do so.

"Nice place," she said as she swung her hips into the room.

Pius chuckled, wondering what sort of temptation this was. He couldn't take his eyes off her body, though. She wore a miniskirt, crop top that exposed her waist and navel, worn under an oversize long-sleeve shirt. Her hair was cut low and dyed blonde. She had several rings in her ears.

"I see you don't recognize me, Mr Pius?"

"I don't," Pius responded. He couldn't fathom how and where he'd ever met her.

The lady glanced over the room, examining everything with rapt detail. The chairs, the bed, the wardrobe, and then the television tuned to CNN.

"Christiane Amanpour! I watched her interview with Israeli Prime Minister, where she analysed Middle East politics. You should see it." She went over to a flower bud beside the TV, stroking her fingers over it.

"Yes, I've seen the highlights," Pius said.

"The highlights do not say much. She did an amazing job there. It means you've not been watching her."

"Not really, I haven't been for quite a while."

"Have you seen her interview with Chimamanda Adichie? It's a blockbuster."

"Really, when was that? I should check it."

"You can get it on YouTube." She was checking out the bed. "I think it's also archived on the CNN website."

"You sound different from the way you look. You look

uncultured but well-informed." Pius had closed the door but hadn't moved farther from where he stood. He couldn't help but follow her movements with his eyes. She seemed rough around the edges, rather excessively wild, but again, smart. He found himself liking her.

"So now I am curious." He walked towards her. "Who are you?"

"I guess you don't recognize me because there weren't any pictures of me in the house. You know me, Mr Pius," she stated softly.

"I don't know you. Why will I lie about that?" Pius said fondly, amazed at how warm he'd become with this strange girl.

"Anyway, I'm Rita. Rita Onu." She smiled and sat down.

"Rita, Chief Onu's daughter?"

"Yes."

"I heard you were in London. When did you come into town and how have you grown so big and so smart, Rita!"

"I'm no kid anymore. I'm a grownup now."

"How did you find out I am lodged in this hotel and the exact room?"

"You know how these things happen. Word gets around." She smiled. "Enough of me. Tell me about yourself. Are you married, any kids, and who's been taking care of this muscular body?" she asked, eyeing the muscles on Pius' arms.

"I'm not married yet."

"Perfect match then. I know you would have noticed I like you." She walked towards Pius.

Pius yearned to grab her, squeeze her, lock his tongue with hers, and just do anything. He sensed that she was carefree and would do practically anything he wanted. She looked like someone with years of experience and skills. But then, even though he wanted her so badly, he found himself pushing her off.

"Rita, you can't do this," he said, wishing he could punch himself for saying that. What sort of stupid person was he?

"Nothing to worry about, Pius, no one will see us. I like you," she said, placing her bare palm on his chest and rubbing on the hairy part.

Pius groaned in pleasure. He wished so badly to grab and lift her off her feet and onto the bed, but again the voice of reason echoed, warning him not to try it.

Don't do that, run from this trouble, she is your client's daughter. She is Chief's only daughter. Don't mix work with pleasure, run!

"I...I... I can't do this," Pius stuttered as he managed to free himself from her grip.

"I'm sorry if I acted so strangely. I'm sorry but I can't help it. I'm pained, deeply pained by the death of my father," Rita intoned as she burst into tears.

"It's okay, Rita. It's okay." Pius got closer and wrapped his arm around her. The succulence of her skin and beautiful fragrance on her struck him, and he wished he could hold her for eternity.

"I do not have any shoulder to cry on. Please, Pius, can you be here for me?" She buried her tearful face in his shoulder.

"Rita, everything will be alright," Pius noticed himself say, warring between listening to what she said and the thought of her body and its warm scent.

"I have no one to run to. My stepmother has been so mean and wicked to me," she cried on.

"Really? She hasn't been there for you since your dad died?"

"Has she ever had time for anyone? You know how that woman disturbed my father. And it's as though his death has given her all the freedom."

"Don't say that. She isn't like that."

Rita broke away from Pius, wiped her tears, and then stretched so she could stare directly at Pius. She was shorter than he was.

"Then, you do not know her," she said. "My stepmother keeps a bevy of young men she sleeps with. She was doing this when my father was alive. He'd caught her on so many occasions. This affected their relationship and he tried everything to stop her, but she wouldn't because she's a bitch. She sleeps around like a whore. My dad was very forgiving; he forgave her even with all these things."

"Really? You don't mean it!" Pius said, unsure of whether to believe what she was saying. He knew he hadn't known the widow for long, and Chief hadn't really said anything about her infidelity, but he remembered the young man he'd seen in her house the day he arrived in Abuja. It kind of made sense. Maybe Rita was telling the truth.

"I'm so lonely, please don't leave me. My stepmother is dangerous. I believe she killed my father."

"How can you say a thing like that?"

"Because I have evidence to prove it. I have her on tape, discussing with one of her lovers the need to get rid of my father. The bitch and her gigolos killed my father." Rita gave out another howl.

"I'm sorry, I'm sorry." Pius drew her close again.

"I want you to work with me. My mother suffered for my father but she didn't live to enjoy her labour. This woman came into the picture and destroyed everything. We used to be a happy family. Please help me," Rita begged.

"But what can I do? I can't do anything, Rita."

"You can do something. You can help me to avenge my father's death."

"Rita, I can't really do anything." The words had come out and he could not take them back. He wished he could have been more diplomatic, but he didn't know how, one of the problems he had was always saying things without mincing words.

"Then let me be. I can't believe you won't help me." Rita started crying again.

"Please stop crying, all will be fine." Pius made to hold Rita, to console her further.

"Leave me! Don't console me," she cried. "Leave me." She walked towards the door.

"Don't leave. It's going to be alright, Rita," Pius said, trying to stop her from leaving.

"How will it be all right if you refuse to help me?" She opened the door and stormed into the corridor.

Pius was going to run after her but then he remembered he was scantily dressed.

CHAPTER 10

Emeka and Tim walked into the court premises together. Tim clutched a brown case file while Emeka helped him carry his backpack filled with books. The neatly ironed black suit, white shirt, and a red tie with black stripes gave Tim the look of a corporate lawyer, and he'd just cut his hair. He had to dress the part, he thought, if he were to attract a new set of clients; after all, he was now his own boss. He'd told Emeka, too, to have a haircut before the next hearing.

"Wear something responsible," he said. He'd given Emeka some clothes, something better than the baggy trousers he always wore. Obediently, Emeka was dressed in a long-sleeved shirt tucked into a pair of blue trousers. If it were not for Tim, he would have worn his baggy shorts and a wrinkly shirt.

It had rained the night before, and the compound was littered with leaves and debris strewn all over; petrichor emanated from the wet grass.

The entrance into the court premises wasn't quite crowded, but there were some people who milled around the doors to each courtroom, standing, chatting, sitting on the benches, and others walking about. Everywhere you looked, there were television crews and cameramen setting up their gadgets. A few who had already set up were videoing as people walked in and out of the courts.

"Why are there so many people in court today, and the cameramen, what are they here for?" Emeka inquired as he readjusted the backpack, trying to catch up with Tim whose pace he struggled to catch up with.

"There seems to be a high-profile case today," Tim stated.

Tim walked into Court 6, with Emeka following. There was another set of cameramen in the court taking pictures and videos of lawyers.

It was 8:32 a.m. Court sat at 9:00 a.m. or soon thereafter. The cameramen were trying to capture as many images as they could before the judge walked in. Once the court commenced sitting, cameras wouldn't be allowed in the courtroom.

"Good morning, Mr Abubakar," Tim called out, as he walked up to the prosecution counsel, who was exchanging pleasantries with other lawyers.

"Good morning, Mr Tim," Mr Abubakar responded. He was in his early fifties; he had put in about eighteen years prosecuting cases, first as a police prosecutor and then as a police counsel. He had an erroneous belief that in recent times, the law school churned out half-baked lawyers. Any young lawyer before him was considered half-baked until proven otherwise. He had viewed Tim in this light, until they met to negotiate Emeka's discharge. Since then, his view of Tim had changed. The young man wasn't so bad after all, he had thought.

Tim remained standing at the left wing of the court, chatting with Mr Abubakar when the bangs announced the Magistrate's emergence. He quickly moved and went to the chair where he kept his backpack.

"The first case on the cause list," the Registrar announced, "Criminal Case for Hearing, between the Commissioner of Police and Yunus Gaddo, Tunde Edun, and Emeka Okoromadu." The clerk handed the file to the magistrate.

Yunus and Tunde were already in the dock. Emeka joined them. It was no less than a rat, a cat, and a dog in one cage. Each looked at the others with hatred, wishing there was an opportunity to attack. Emeka wanted to direct a fist at Tunde's protruding belly but he let the thought slide.

"Appearances!"

"With utmost humility to this Honourable Court, I am A. Abubakar Esq, for the prosecution."

"May it please Your Worship, Bulus N. Bulus Esq, for the First Defendant, Your Worship."

"May it please Your Worship, Tim Akpan Esq, for the Third Defendant."

"Is that all the parties?" The magistrate inquired.

"Your Worship, there has been a new development. The prosecution was able to apprehend the Second Defendant who was in the wind. We also wish to discharge the Third Defendant, bearing in mind the turn of events."

"Is that so, Mr Abubakar? Then, the Third Defendant has to be properly discharged. Do you have any application before this court to strike out the Third Defendant? The Second Defendant, is he in court?"

"Yes, Your Worship." Mr Abubakar pointed to Tunde, who was handcuffed in the dock.

"Your Worship, that is the Second Defendant, Tunde Edun.

"Uncuff him," The magistrate ordered. One of the policemen who had brought Tunde into court went over to where he was standing and tried to uncuff Tunde. It took a while, as though he wasn't sure of the right key.

"Prosecutor, you should never bring a defendant before me chained like an animal. What is your name?" the magistrate asked, as he continued writing.

"Tunde Edun."

"Do you speak and understand English?"

"Yes, I do."

The magistrate ordered the charge be read, and it was read.

"Do you understand what was read to you?" The magistrate inquired.

"Yes, I do," Tunde answered, looking down.

"Are you guilty or not guilty?"

"I am not guilty," he mumbled.

"Your Worship, having pleaded not guilty, we shall take a date to continue with the trial. We however have an application before Your Worship," Mr Abubakar said.

"Before that, Mr Edun, do you have a lawyer?" The magistrate asked.

"No, I don't," Tunde stated.

"It is your legal right to be represented by a lawyer. Before the next adjourned date, you should get a lawyer."

"Okay, My Lord," Tunde responded.

"Mr Abubakar, wait a minute, let me record you. Your application is dated?" The magistrate asked while she searched for the document in the case file before her.

"Your Worship, it's an application dated the tenth of July. It is praying that this Honourable Court to strike off the name of the Third Defendant in this suit."

"Any objection to the application?" The magistrate asked.

"No objection," Tim and Bulus chorused, and Abubakar continued, "Your Worship, our application is supported by a nine-paragraph affidavit sworn to by one Mr Itodo Okayi."

"Please move in terms, Mr Abubakar. You can see I have some high profile matters today. I want the criminal matters dispensed with so we can take civil matters."

The court granted the application. Emeka Okoromadu's name was struck out from the charge.

Emeka ran out towards Tim. He was shouting and almost screaming.

The magistrate struck the gavel on her desk.

"Order! Order! Order in my court. Mr Tim, call your client to order. The court is still sitting," the magistrate warned sternly.

Emeka quickly knelt down begging. At this point a police orderly approached to restrain him.

"Your Worship, I'm deeply sorry. I warned my client several times that the court is not a place to make noise or shout as he is doing. I believe he got excited and forgot all I'd told him. May Your Worship not hold the folly of my client against him," Tim pleaded.

"Orderly, let him be. You can get up Mr Emeka and go out. You can jubilate as you wish outside my courtroom."

"Thank you, Ma. Thank you, My Worship. Oh Lord, thank you," Emeka intoned, afraid to say more.

"Mr Abubakar, I suppose you aren't continuing today?"

"No, Your Worship, we shall take a date to continue with the trial. We have another witness to also call aside from the ones listed."

"Take a date."

Mr Abubakar and Mr Bulus quickly examined their diaries and agreed on a date. They informed the clerk who confirmed that the date was suitable for the court.

"This matter is adjourned to the twenty-fourth of July for hearing," the magistrate stated.

Tim, with all the other counsel in the matter, first bowed. Emeka bowed, and they left the courtroom, Tunde and Yunus angrily glanced at Emeka as they were led to a waiting prison van.

CHAPTER 11

For the second time, Pius attempted to sneak out of his hotel room. Each time, he'd turn the doorknob to go but lost his nerve. He knew no one would stop him and no one was watching, yet he couldn't get himself to leave.

He'd been cooped up for over a week, since he arrived in Abuja. He'd only gone out when Nick came to pick him up. The only other time had been when he hung out with Thara. He had been a hostage, caged by his thoughts and fears of his past catching up with him. He watched CNN, listened to music, seen movies, read magazines, and yet something was missing – FOOTBALL. The cable TV in the room only had select channels and the leagues weren't connected. He had complained and was told the room's subscription didn't cover matches. The hotel was renovating its viewing centre, and it would be ready in about a week. Guests were encouraged to watch the matches at the hotel viewing bar where they could buy drinks. He thought the hotel management were so wrong. They were right about only one thing: the drinks. Football wasn't a game you watched alone. It wasn't a game you would enjoy unaccompanied by a bottle of beer.

Pius sat on the edge of his bed. He was wearing an Adidas

tracksuit and his club jersey. He was tired of everything. The fact
that he couldn't even step into the hotel lobby, use the pool or
the gym, troubled him deeply. It felt worse than being a criminal
on house arrest.

Perhaps he would check out and opt for a low-budget hotel
where he believed his detractors would most likely not frequent.
But then he thought, what would he tell Madam was his reason
for leaving the hotel? And if he did that, he was sure he would
have to pay for the bills, thereby depleting his meagre resources.
No! He quickly ditched the idea.

Madam had told him not to worry about anything. Anytime
he needed to step out, all he had to do was to dial a number.
Nick and the driver would come and take him wherever he desired. But which man would do such a thing? It was like handing
over his freedom. He was always in the room and the few times
Nick had come around, unannounced, he'd met him. Madam
and Nick believed that he stayed true to the instruction but, unknown to Madam, anxiety had kept him locked up.

He looked at his jersey, the Chelsea insignia prominent on it.
His love for the club was beyond comprehension; it was second
to nothing.

"No, I can't miss this Chelsea match," he said to himself.

He got up, picked his phone, the new iPhone he'd gone
to buy at Emab Plaza with Nick, and walked to the door. He
opened the door, removed the room card from the wall socket,
and everything in the room went dark. He stepped out, tossed
the card in his hip pocket, and jammed the door.

In the hallway, two doors away from his, a boy and a girl
grappled at each other. They were hugging, cuddling, and kissing
at the same time. The boy looked about 19 years old, and the girl
was not more than 17. University students, you would say. The
boy, despite his dreadlocks, gold chains, and saggy jeans almost

slipping off his waist, gave off the appearance of easy money. The girl, on the other hand, looked very much responsible.

Pius stared hard at them. He hissed and gasped at how bad things had changed. Twenty-year-olds, lodging in hotels to do this.

The most annoying part was that the love birds didn't notice him. If they did, they didn't care. The boy emptied the contents of his pocket – car key, a cigarette pack, dollar and naira bills, some cards as he hurriedly searched for something, perhaps the room card. As Pius walked past them, his eyes met that of the girl, and she looked away. You could tell she still had some innocence, unlike the boy.

Pius strode on the red rug that stretched through the doorway and farther down the stairs to the hotel lobby. The hotel lobby was an open space crowded with bodies, as though an event was ongoing in one of the halls. There were people all over the place, most of them talking to one another.

He meandered through the crowd, avoiding eye contact in case he bumped into someone he knew. He was trying so hard to get to the reception desk unnoticed.

"Where can someone watch football here?" he asked one of the receptionists. A young guy stood in between two ladies, one answering the phone and the other chewing gum, her eyes roving over the crowd.

"Sorry, sir, we have a place here but it isn't open. They are renovating it."

"Damn it! I know that," he retorted. "Tell me where else outside the hotel."

"There is Tropicana Garden about five blocks away from the hotel gate. It's an open recreational centre that has a viewing centre."

"I want a local place."

"It's local, sir."

"Are the hotel cabs available at this time?"

"They are. Once you step out of the lobby and into the garage, you will see them."

Pius thanked him and disappeared into the crowd. He moved as swiftly as he could until he was completely outside the lobby, out of sight of prying eyes.

The evening breeze outside first greeted him. It was soothing and refreshing, very much unlike the air-conditioning in his hotel room. The skies were lit with the rising moon cut in half and with a splatter of stars shining far off. He looked up, inhaling the evening breeze into his starving lungs.

"*Oga, you wan commot?*" Two cab drivers ran towards him, each trying to convince him to follow him and not the other.

"*Oga*, come with me. Don't mind him," a stout, aged man shouted.

"Old wrinkled man, you won't mind your business. *Oga*, follow me. Don't mind him," the younger man countered.

"Young man, be careful because he who mocks an elder may never be fortunate to experience old age. The wrinkle is amongst the fragrance of old age."

"*Papa*, where is your car?" Pius asked. He didn't like the way the young men made his age an issue.

Elated, the man walked Pius to a car parked three miles away. Each time they got to a painted taxi, Pius stopped, thinking it was his car, but the man would shake his head and beg him to continue. Other drivers tried calling Pius to leave the man and enter their vehicle. Pius ignored them and followed the man.

The old man's car was a Toyota Camry 2000. The car was well worn out and unfit for a hotel taxi. Only one reason could come to mind why the car was still allowed by the hotel management

– an act of pity for the man. It was the same pity for the old man that made Pius leave better cars to enter the rickety thing.

"*Oga*, enter." The driver opened the back door for Pius to climb in. Pius sat on the edge of the seat. The man slammed the door, but it didn't lock. He slammed it harder again, making so much noise. It stayed closed this time.

He turned to the driver's seat and squeezed himself behind the wheel. As though the car had no ignition key, he pulled out two wires, setting them together. The car first sputtered before the engine came alive.

"Tropicana Garden," Pius said to the old man struggling with the paddles and the gear to get the car in motion. It jerked, wobbled, jerked again before it coughed into life.

***

Tropicana Garden bustled with activities as Pius arrived. He paid the old man and hopped out of the taxi. The viewing centre was an open space with several trees providing shade. Plastic tables, arranged with rubber chairs, filled the arena with each table seating five or six occupants. The viewers had turned their seats so each table faced the direction of the TV sets. The waiters walked over to the tables, taking empty bottles and replacing them with more drinks as the football enthusiasts drank, chatted, and screamed at each goal attempt. Gigantic speakers projected the sound.

Pius walked through the spaces between the tables, glancing furtively to see if there were available seats. Because the match had begun, everywhere was fully occupied. As he walked, he avoided eye contact, certain that he wouldn't meet anyone who knew him in such a place. Yet, he didn't take any chances. Every now and then, he saw an empty seat, but when he moved to grab it, he was told the occupant had stepped away and would be back. He walked through little spaces until he got to a place closer to the projector.

"Can I sit here?" he asked the occupants of the table.

"Yes, you can," a young man sitting next to the empty seat said.

"Go, go! Score the ball, you idiot. Can you imagine he missed that goal?" He'd already turned his attention away from Pius as he screamed.

"What's the score line?" Pius asked.

"Three-two, Chelsea is leading," one of the other occupants stated.

It was Chelsea against Liverpool. The echo of the Stamford Bridge fans and British commentators from the loudspeakers could be heard miles away. You had to yell loudly to someone who must also make an effort and pay close attention to hear you. It was usually the same with most local viewing centres.

"What would you like to have, sir?" A lady bearing a tray of drinks asked.

"What do you have?" Pius asked, surprised that the waiter hadn't noticed the table already filled with drinks.

"Drinks on me, sir," someone on the table said. "Waiter, bring more drinks for this table," he continued, pointing at some empty bottles.

"Replace these bottles on the table. We are winning this match." The young man was also wearing a Chelsea jersey. It was obvious he controlled the table.

Pius thanked him and opened one of the bottles of Star Lager Beer. He poured himself some.

"A football magician, filing straight." The British commentator's voice boomed through the speakers.

"He passes the ball to Rodriguez.

"Rodriguez gives a header to Hazard.

"Eden Hazard filing straight to the midfield.

"Hazard is up, up against the goalkeeper.

"Oh no! Wait a minute. It's a…a…!"

The entire place erupted.

"Goooooooooooooal! Goal! Goal!"

You could hear similar choruses from viewing centers miles away. There was jubilation on the tables and because there were more Chelsea fans, the noise quietened the Liverpool fans. Some people left their seats, glasses of beer in hand, running up and about, screaming. Someone had just hugged Pius, spilling his drink. The seats and tables had been disorganized in the whole imbroglio.

Pius was standing, screaming *"Ole Ole Ole Ole…"* repeating the same chant resonating in Stamford Bridge. Because he wore his club jersey, it gave him away so easily, and every now and then he was slapped on the back or hugged by someone wearing a similar jersey, some of whom had come running from other tables.

"An unbelievable goal," the commentator continued as the place calmed.

"Taking the Blues to a comfortable win. Four-two with a comfortable two-goal lead against Liverpool! What a fantastic finishing! Twenty-one minutes to the end of the match."

Pius, like the other fans, had returned to his drink. He was on his second bottle. Some efforts had been made at rearranging the seats and tables but much couldn't be achieved. The sitting arrangements were altered. A lady selling pepper soup and fresh fish had come by the table, and Pius had ordered fish and pepper soup for the table. He'd been told the price was N500 and N3,500 could go round for everyone.

"Excuse me. I think I *sabi* you?"

Pius turned to see who tapped on his shoulder.

"I don't think so," he replied, frowning at the young man standing beside him. He was sitting at a table that had just been arranged to face Pius' table.

"I'm sure. Barrister Pius." The young man pointed. Surprisingly, he had been one of those who had run to hug Pius a moment ago.

"No," Pius said, but he wasn't firm.

"It's you. Oh my God, *you dey alive!*" The guy screamed and came closer.

"I be Jonathan, Mr Solomon's driver. Solomon Edeh."

Oh no, not again, Pius thought. Could he ever step out in this town without being noticed?

"I go call my *Oga*. I'm doing so now," Jonathan said animatedly.

And before Pius could stop him, Jonathan was on the phone with his boss.

CHAPTER 12

Solomon Edeh banged his fists on the table and yelled, "She can't sack us just like that. We had an employment agreement with the company, and I read online that where there is any agreement, they can't sack the employees."

"That's not true. My lawyer friend who I asked said that it depends on the clauses in the employment contract and letter of employment. He said ordinarily, he who can hire can fire and after I gave him our agreement, he said the company can fire us. The only requirement was to ensure the company followed the agreement and the extant labour laws and according to him the notice period for workers five years and above is a month's notice and that is what they have given us," someone at the table added.

"We are not letting this go like this." Solomon said.

"But what can we do? As directed, the MD sent the circular to us, giving us the notice. What can we really do?" another employee at the table asked.

It was a meeting of the employees of Onu Group of Companies, four of them whose employments were about to be terminated. One employee had called the others and in a few minutes, they had secured an exclusive table in the private bar. The discussion was about their survival. It was not a fun meeting, and when a lady had come to ask what drinks they would like to have, they waved her away. None of them were in the mood for drinks. Any attempt to drink would take them into the realm of intoxication. Each one of them had bitterness visible on his face.

"Chief wouldn't have done this if he were alive," Solomon stated.

"And now, he's dead. His wife has taken over."

"Can't we stop her? She can't suddenly terminate our employment after we've spent years building the company with Chief."

"What we should be talking about is not whether she can terminate our employments. As you already know, it is as good as done," a fifty-four-year-old man amongst them pointed out.

"What do you mean?" Solomon asked him.

"What we should be talking about is how we should secure our benefits. We must fight for our benefits. Segun, can we get your lawyer friend to help us? The problem with lawyers is that they can't help you without asking for their fees."

"Old man, I'm not ready to retire now. What benefits?" Solomon asked.

"You will lose it all if you don't get a lawyer."

"Who said that?" Solomon cut in. He dominated the discussion. He turned to the others to see who would jettison the idea the old man had proposed and side with him.

Suddenly, his phone rang.

"What is it, Jonathan? I told you I'm in a meeting. Watch the football match. I will call you to bring the car when I'm done," he said.

"No, sir. *I get urgent thing I wan tell you.*"

"What is it?"

"*I been see Barrister Pius.* You remember Barrister Pius Egbe?"

Solomon went cold, paused before asking, "What sort of joke is that? Have you had too much beer? Which Pius are you talking about? The man that is dead."

"*He dey here. I dey here with him, sir.*"

"What? Where did you say you are?"

"*We dey* Tropicana, sir. It's the viewing centre, *wey dey* two blocks from the guest house where you *dey* get your meeting."

"Which side of the Tropicana are you?"

"Where *them dey* watch football match. We *dey* beside the projector setting, sir."

"Stay there. Don't lose him. Stay there, we are coming."

Solomon ended the call and turned to face the others.

"Guys, wait. We will treat this matter later. We have another issue at hand."

"What is it? What could be more pressing than losing your job? Is your wife in labour?"

"This is more like it," Solomon said. "Do you guys remember Barrister Pius?"

"Yes. Chief's former lawyer. The one we gave six million naira each and he suddenly died with no means to retrieve our money?"

"Yes. It seems he isn't dead at all. If what my driver is saying is true, he is three blocks away from us."

"What? And you are still sitting down?" The fifty-four-year-old man inquired.

They stood up hastily and rushed out of the guesthouse.

***

Pius realised the moment Jonathan recognized him that he now had an issue. He began to get a sinking feeling when Jonathan made a call, presumably to his boss, Solomon Edeh. He lost interest in the game. Chelsea was winning, and it was a few minutes to the end of the match. He had never loved and missed his hotel room as much as he did in that moment.

When he got up to say he was going to use the restroom,

Jonathan had also gotten up to say he would like to use the restroom. Some young men at the same table with Jonathan had
gotten up to follow them. He thought of running, but then he
knew even if he outran Jonathan, he couldn't outrun the men.
He dismissed the thought. The men could attempt to lynch him
if he tried to run. It would take only a shout of "Thief!" and he
would be beaten and perhaps set ablaze.

He began to think of how many times he'd warned himself
not to go out. How many times he'd resisted the urge to leave
his hotel room. But for the love for football, he thought. With
each passing second, he knew he was running out of options. He
walked up to Jonathan.

"Please, can you let me go?"

"Barrister, *you know say I no hold you,*" Jonathan replied. "*We
only ask make you wait and see my boss. He dey road dey come
meet you.*"

"I know that. I will give you anything. Tell him the person
you saw wasn't me. Name your price please."

"Price? Sir, *you wan make kasala burst here? You think sey I fit
tell my boss that kind nonsense? Do you know how many times him
don wish you dey alive to return him money?*"

"I don't know."

"And how many times him *don wish say* you rot in hell?"

"He said that?"

"Sir, *please no talk like say you no sabi my boss.* Please sit down.
He go soon reach here."

Solomon and the others arrived just as the match ended.
Their anxious eyes darted all over the place as they looked for
Pius. Jonathan spotted them and waved them over.

"Barrister Pius! So a dead man can live again," Solomon said.
He looked at Pius. He'd grown thin and feeble. His skin looked

darker and his hair looking unkempt. A lot had changed about his look, but you would still know he was the one.

"Welcome, Mr Edeh. Good evening Mr Patrick, Mr Segun, and Mr Sani. We have been waiting for you," Pius replied, barely able to look at their faces.

"You are not the one who has been waiting. We have been waiting for you for three years," Patrick, the fifty-four-year-old man fired back.

"How do we explain this? Three years ago, you were dead. Confirmed dead with your car burnt and your body in your car. There were eyewitnesses who confirmed that. You were buried and now you are here. Tell us how true the saying is that dead people come back to life," Mr Solomon queried.

"I don't know how to explain it," Pius said.

"What's there to explain, it's simple. You tricked us all into believing you were dead. You vanished with our money and the only thing that you could think of was to frame your own death. Ah! Pius you are wicked," Mr Segun said.

Solomon came closer and grabbed Pius by the shirt.

"Where is our money? We do not want the property anymore. Where is the six million naira I gave you three years ago? It would have interest, at least, of three million naira. So we are talking about nine million naira."

"Mr Solomon, you are choking me. Can we step out and talk?" Pius pleaded, noticing that more people had gathered around them.

"There is no going anywhere. Ah! Ah! We are not going anywhere," Mr Segun added.

"Walai, I want to know how he did it. Barrister, explain to us what really happened."

"Ah, what's there to explain, Sani? A man duped us, and you are telling him to explain."

"So what? I want him to explain, I have a right to know," Mr Sani stated angrily. "Go ahead."

"I collected your money to buy the properties," Pius began.

"We know all that," Mr Solomon interrupted.

"*Gaskia*, Solo, let the man explain."

"It wasn't only your money that I had. I had also collected seventy million naira from a client and another eighty-two million naira from someone else and another…"

"Sani, you see what I'm telling you," Solomon interjected. "This man wants to keep wasting our time."

"Ah! Why can't you go straight to the point?" Patrick retorted.

"Sorry, sorry. I collected the money, and the day before I was to make payment to the estate, someone I knew that was well to do, came to me with an investment opportunity. He said it was Forex trading and if I put in five million naira, I would receive ten million naira within seven days. He showed me their track record and all that."

"So you collected our money meant for real estate and put it there?"

"I first put in the five million naira I had with me to see if it truly worked. Seven days after I received ten million naira. It was after that I started putting pressure on you to pay up, on the basis that the price of the property was going to go up in about a week."

"You pressured us to pay you so you could use the money for your money-doubling scheme?"

"Yes."

"How much did you put in?"

"All of it, including other huge sums I collected from other clients."

"I don't believe you," Segun stated. "Even if you are telling the truth, that's your business. What we know is that we each gave you six million naira to buy properties for us which we never received to date."

"Even if what you are saying is true, what happened to the guys you gave the money?" Solomon asked.

"They vanished. It dawned on me that they were scammers immediately I made the huge payment to them."

"So when we started disturbing you, you faked your own death?"

"That was the only thing I could do. The pressure was so much. I knew if I hadn't faked my death, I would have still died somehow. Death was my only path to survival."

"You are about to die a real death now," Mr Solomon stated, laughing.

"Whose body did you use in the vehicle?" Mr Sani asked.

"It was the body of an armed robber who was gunned down by policemen. I had a top police official arrange it for me."

"And the police report came back that it was you. You dressed him in your clothes, chain, and ring. There were even eyewitnesses to the incident."

"All that was arranged."

"Wow!"

"A service of song was held at your place and burial conducted at the Gudu cemetery. You want us to believe that you watched yourself being buried?"

"What happened to your properties? Your house and every other thing?"

"It was nothing compared to the investments I had made. I knew I was dealing with scary people. First, I knew it was against our rules as lawyers to use clients' monies for personal benefit. Once that money was gone, I knew it was my undoing because some of the clients threatened to report me to the Legal Practitioners Disciplinary Committee. I also know some of the clients would rather want me dead."

"I heard you also duped Don Bruno, the drug baron?"

"I put his money in the same investment."

"Where have you been all these years? In heaven or hell? Obviously hell, because you do not deserve heaven," Mr Segun stated.

"I've been in Lagos."

"Enough of this bullshit. Let us take this guy to the police station to give us our money," Mr Patrick interrupted.

"Who is talking of the police? We won't do that. He gives us the money now or we take care of him ourselves," Mr Solomon fumed. Jonathan with his men muttered in agreement.

"Such a man doesn't deserve to live," an onlooker added.

"I am sorry. I am truly sorry," Pius pleaded.

"That's why we need to send him back to hell. A lawyer, for that matter?"

"I am deeply sorry for the pains…"

"You can't be. We just lost our jobs and our lives are in shambles."

"You lost your job with Onu Group?" Pius asked, looking for a new lead that could save him.

"Are you even aware that Chief is dead?" Mr Sani asked.

"And not your kind of death. He died and is in the morgue," Mr Segun said.

"Yes, I am aware. Madam called me to come to Abuja, which is why I left Lagos and I'm here."

"Madam knew you were alive and knew how to reach you all along?" Mr Sani asked.

"Yes."

"I knew that woman was evil," Mr Patrick added.

"Do you need to be told? It would take an evil person to direct that staff be laid off for no given reason. It's not as though the company is experiencing any problems." Solomon concurred.

"Can I please help?"

"Help with what?" Sani asked.

"You are not helping with anything. We want our money and nothing else."

"Let us hear what he has to say," Mr Segun interrupted.

"Can I talk to Madam Jennifer about your dismissal? I can help get your jobs back."

"You aren't doing that. We won't allow you," Mr Solomon answered.

"Solo, you were arguing earlier that you don't want to leave the job. What if he can do something?"

"This rogue? Do something? Are you guys so rash as to let him dupe you a second time? I want the job but not from him. Period!"

"He has to take us to Madam then and convince her, whichever way he would. That's not our business," Mr Sani stated.

"Are we going to let him go before?" Mr Patrick inquired.

"What happens to our money?" Mr Segun asked.

"We will hold him to that after, but if he could make Madam direct the MD to reverse our dismissal, then that's something," said Mr Sani.

"We will agree on one condition," Mr Solomon said after thinking through what others had said. "We will go with you to Madam and you promise that there and then she will reverse our sack."

"Yes, that is fine."

"You will still pay us our money"

"Yes I will. I will. But please could you people give me some time to pay up after I help with your job?"

"That is okay," Mr Sani answered.

They followed Pius as he led the way to see Mrs Jennifer.

CHAPTER 13

The evening air was clean and crisp. The room was airy, probably because the building had no true windows. The makeshift carton paper and plywood used on the window spaces barely covered anything. The feel of the room could also be attributed to the frequent rainfall. Either way, it helped douse the effects of heat.

Emeka lay on a wooden bench, face up. He wasn't alone. He had the company of Onoja, Ike, and Dogo. Onoja was sleeping. At 6:32 p.m., he had slid beneath the mosquito net. He slept early, soon he would be snoring.

Emeka had joined them as soon as he was released from prison. He had lost his job as a security guard and couldn't return to the yard. He couldn't afford to rent a place either. Onoja, who he had worked with in a block industry before his job as a guard, had come to see his cousin at the prison the day Emeka was released. Onoja had offered him a place. He said it was somewhere Emeka could manage until he found his footing. Emeka had agreed and when his lawyer asked if he had a place, he had said yes. Unknown to Emeka, the place had no windows or doors and the floor and walls weren't even plastered.

Emeka looked at the ceiling. The black polythene and pieces

of cement bag hanging off the roof fluttered. The rest of what was supposed to be the ceiling was covered with nails and cobwebs. He looked down towards Ike's greasy, dirty clothes – work clothes hanging on nails fixed to the wall. The clean clothes hung on a rope. Onoja and Dogo didn't mix their used clothes with Ike's mechanic clothes; rather, they were in a heap on one side of the room. Emeka kept all his clothes in his bags.

They were all in the sitting room of a three-bedroom apartment on the first floor. It was a block of flats. They had a neighbour on the ground floor whose wife just gave birth to a baby girl. Since Emeka moved in, he hadn't seen the landlord, and in fact none of the others had seen him. The building wasn't only unfinished, it was also abandoned.

"*Walai*, any time I tune to news *for* this country, I *dey vex*," Dogo stated. He held his tiny receiver radio to his ears as he lay on a mat next to Ike.

"Is that BBC Hausa? What are they saying?" Ike asked.

"I don't even get it. *Kawai*, there are so many bad news everywhere," Dogo stated in his deep Hausa accent.

"That's Nigeria for you," Emeka added as he clapped his hands in an effort to kill a mosquito. He missed.

"What is it with this your clapping, Emeka? You won't let me listen to the news, *ko?*"

"Dogo, aren't you seeing the mosquitoes? I don't know the kind of body you guys have."

"Dogo, don't mind Emeka. He's acting as though he will die if a mosquito bites him. Let them bite. You will take malaria meds afterwards, it will not kill you."

"I don't just like their buzzing sound," Emeka clapped again as he tried to hit another mosquito. He missed again.

"It can be frustrating, I know," Ike said. "But thank God we are on the first floor and you know mosquitoes don't fly that high. Imagine what mama baby downstairs and her kids would be going through. The new-born baby."

"I can't even think about it."

"Emeka, *na ajebo* you be."

"Oh yes. Billionaire *pikin*. When are you meeting your other family?"

"I've told you people not to call me that. I'm not even sure if the family will be happy to meet me."

"Why won't they?" Ike asked.

"Don't mind him," Dogo added and dropped his radio. "This news is annoying me. Emeka, you don't beg for what is yours, you take it."

"But how do I take it? My lawyer and his security friend said I need my mother to get through with this and I don't know how to deal with her."

"How to deal with your mother? This boy truly needs some sense."

"This *aboki*. You won't let me be? It is only the wearer of a shoe that can tell where it pinches."

"Why would I? You have started with your proverbs. It is your people that say that only a fool stands in the river while soap lather troubles his eyes. Look at this one living in an uncompleted building, and if he wasn't fanning himself, he would be battling mosquitoes. When he should have been thinking of how to take hold of the key to his father's wealth and fortune. Just know that you have no option than to give me the contract to supply the rugs in your house when you build it. You know I can deal in these things." Dogo looked straight at Emeka.

"Igbo man in Hausa body. Core business boy," Emeka joked.

"*Nna men*. You can say that again, I lived in Onitsha for several years and one thing I learnt is that wisdom is not determined by the size of one's head, nor is it peculiar to a tribe."

"As in, this Dogo beats me. Sometimes I wonder the kind of sense he has. Abeg, Emeka *na* me go do your house POP!" Ike added.

"You people are here apportioning the jobs you will do in my house. I laugh at your enthusiasm."

"You better believe in the power of your tongue, Emeka. My father usually said that to me," Ike added.

"Don't mind him. What is stopping you?"

"My mother!" Emeka screamed as he turned and sat on the bench. Ike and Dogo got up and joined him.

Emeka had come to enjoy their company and night after night, they stayed up late to tattle endlessly about life. Besides Onoja, who slept very early, the three of them were night owls. The first few nights, Emeka wasn't very happy Onoja went to bed so early. Sometimes, he would nod off while they talked. He had asked and Ike said it was because of the nature of his job. He was a motor mechanic and usually came back to the house dirty and tired.

That wasn't enough of an excuse, Emeka thought. After all, the others were also handy men. Ike fixed POP while Dogo sold fabrics on a wheelbarrow. Those were taxing also but none of them slept the way Onoja did.

Onoja was Emeka's friend from the onset and was the one that brought him to the house but over time, he had also become fond of Dogo and Ike. The gist made them bond so well. Some nights, it would be Dogo telling stories of his encounters as he sold fabrics in Onitsha. Other nights, Ike talked about his day, what happened at the construction site, while Emeka shared his prison experiences, his court case, and how he had discovered he had a billionaire father.

"How is your mother preventing you, Emeka?" Dogo asked.

"I can't see myself forgiving her," Emeka responded.

"I'm going to the kitchen to get some water," Ike moved away.

Dogo came closer to Emeka, tapped him on the shoulder, and said, "The mother's hand that pets a child when he does good is the same that spank him when he does wrong. Your mother did whatever she did out of love."

"Love, you said? I didn't do anything to her, Dogo. What wrong could I have done to her as a baby? Was it my offence that she conceived me out of wedlock, what was my crime for her to abandon me as she did?"

"I can't tell. I really can't tell, Emeka, but what I can say is that you have to forgive her. That's the only way you can find peace." said Dogo.

"It pains me so much," Emeka answered.

"I understand how painful that could be. Let me tell you a story. You often tell me that I act like Igbo people. The truth is that my father was a military man. He was redeployed to several parts of Nigeria, until he was sent to Onitsha where he spent most of his career. The way we moved determined how I changed schools. My mother died when I was two and my father married my stepmother. You know in Islamic culture, my father could have married more than one wife, but he loved my mother so much he couldn't marry another. He married my stepmother to take care of me but she hated me. When she gave birth to my step-brothers and sisters she turned me into a servant. My father was always busy, and he didn't know what was going on in the house. When I tried to complain to my father, my stepmom warned that she would kill me if I did."

"That's disturbing!"

"If I show you my back, you will see the scars her injuries caused me."

"What?"

"I was so hurt and abused growing up. I was traumatized. My

father sent me to the best school in Onitsha, because he wanted me to be a lawyer. I went to Onitsha Unity School."

"Do you want some water?" Ike shouted from the kitchen.

"No, I don't," Dogo responded and continued. "My education was cut short when my father died. When I couldn't bear the torture anymore, I ran away from home and stayed with a Mallam selling fabrics in Onitsha main market."

"When you left the house, she didn't look for you?"

"I don't know. If she did, it would have been to enslave me further. I served the Mallam for six years and after my service, he gave me money to set up my own business."

"What about your stepmother?" Ike asked, as he re-joined the conversation.

"I didn't hear from her again. After I finished my apprenticeship with the Mallam, I went to Kano to take a wife. I met her again with my other siblings. She'd relocated to Kano."

"And I hope you gave her evil for her evil?" Emeka asked.

"I had so much heaviness in my heart when I met her. I'd sworn to do that, but I discovered I couldn't. I found myself forgiving her."

"You did what?" Emeka asked.

"I forgave her. To be candid, I haven't felt any less peaceful since I did. The Holy Quran says, the reward of evil is evil thereof, but whoever forgives and makes amends, his reward is from God."

"I can't imagine myself forgiving such," Emeka stated.

"I'm finding it difficult to understand also," Ike added.

"Emeka, do you feel some burden in your heart whenever you remember your mother?" Dogo asked.

"Yes I do. I feel terrible at the thought of her."

"That is what unforgiveness does. It eats at your heart and keeps you angry anytime you remember the person. But always remember that no matter how smelly a carcass has become, it is still a good meal to the vulture. Everything just like everyone has the good and the ugly."

"What you are saying is true," Ike agreed.

"Every one of us has good and bad sides. I understand you may not have spent time with her as a baby, but the fact that she didn't abort you and she didn't throw you away as a baby also meant she had a good side. When we remember the good side of people that hurt us, it helps us to forgive them. To be candid, it is to our own good to forgive. The pain that comes with unforgiveness yields no profit. I've been there. I can tell you," Dogo said as he tapped Emeka and continued.

"I don't think what your mother did can be compared to my stepmother, but I forgave her. I send her money from time to time and my wife, who is in Kano, also goes to see her from time to time."

"Thank you, Dogo," Emeka said.

"It seems when someone forgives, he sees a reason to start again," Ike added.

"Very true. When I lost my shop to fire in Onitsha because my boy forgot to turn off the boiling ring he used to make tea, I couldn't find any way to forgive him. I couldn't start again. It was after I forgave him that I found the courage to move to Abuja and start all over again."

"Wow! It was your boy that caused the fire that razed your shop?"

"Yes. *Walai*, I almost died. It was after I forgave him that I found peace again. The peace to start afresh. Emeka, you see why you need to forgive your mother?"

"Thank you, Dogo. Thank you so much. I will find a way."

"You have to because as I said, I'm going to be the one to supply the rugs for your house."

CHAPTER 14

Mr Solomon and Pius were in the car driven by Jonathan. Mr Sani and Segun were in the other car. The boys with Jonathan were in Mr Patrick's car.

The drive from Tropicana to Chief Onu's house in Asokoro which would have been five minutes took about thirty-three minutes. It would have been a shorter drive. But Pius, who was directing Jonathan, didn't know that a shorter route to Asokoro had just been commissioned, the Goodluck Ebele Express road. They were caught up in the evening traffic.

The evening traffic was building. Most of the vehicles going to Nyanya and Mararaba would have to pass through Asokoro to get to Nyanya. This caused heavy traffic. A large percentage of workers in Abuja live in the outskirts – Kubwa, Dutse, Mararaba, Kuje, Gwagwalada, so each morning everyone hit the road to the city centre and in the evenings, used the same road back home. Usually the rush hour began by 4:00 p.m. and ran into late evening sometimes.

As the car slowed down in the traffic, Pius looked ahead to see the long queue stretching the farthest his eyes could see.

"This traffic is really heavy," he said, wondering when Abuja roads became like Lagos'.

"This road be *no dey* like this," Jonathan said.

"Why is it not moving? It's like Lagos traffic." Pius looked at the back seat only to find Mr Solomon fuming.

"Buy your gala," a hawker shouted, as he shoved his snacks through the window of the car.

"Get that thing out of here now," Mr Solomon shouted from the back seat.

"Bottled water. Buy your cold bottle water," another hawker screamed towards Mr Solomon. He shouted again.

"Jonathan, roll up the glass!" Mr Solomon screamed after he tried to do so and it didn't budge.

Pius looked at the army of hawkers moving from car to car trying to sell their goods. He wondered how they made a living. Some of them were teenagers and the others selling caps, power banks, and newspapers were in their twenties and early thirties. All of the goods for each trader put together couldn't add up to a hundred USD. How much could such a person sell in a day?

After a long wait, the cars in front began to move. Jonathan tapped the pedal and they moved as well. A siren blared from behind. A government official trying to barge through the traffic. His security detail had left the car and walked forward, directing other cars to clear a path.

"Leave road come go where?" Jonathan said quietly, so the military man wouldn't hear him. The man in military uniform had tapped his car and moved forward to the next car.

The siren kept blaring but the cars remained in the same spot. Not that the drivers didn't want to move the cars off the road, but there was really nowhere to move to as the road was entirely occupied.

Jonathan kept forcing the car through using any little opportunity he got. Every other driver did the same. You wouldn't really be able to drive in such traffic if you didn't know how to drive.

Car horns blared as drivers tried not to be run over by others.

A boy selling Gala had been hit by a vehicle. He was unconscious, his goods strewn all over the road. Police at the scene and medics from Road Safety Corp struggled to resuscitate him before taking him away in the ambulance. The boy was bleeding profusely; his blood was all over the place.

Police controlled the traffic as more people stopped their cars. Jonathan wanted to stop but Mr Solomon told him to continue moving. The policemen soon created a little opening. The cars parked at both ends of the road had formed a bottleneck. Some of the boys selling had also gathered, wishing and praying the injured boy survived. A few others went on with hawking their things as there were more people in the traffic.

"What a pity," Pius said as the car went through the crowd.

* * *

Mrs Jennifer Onu was in her sitting room when Pius and the others arrived. It was a few minutes past 7 p.m. She'd told the gate man to let them in anytime they arrived.

She'd just tucked in her son, Junior, into bed and was walking into the second sitting room upstairs when Nick came to inform her that Pius was around.

"Where is he?" she asked.

"They are in the central sitting room."

"They? You mean he's not alone?" asked Jennifer. She had received a call from Pius saying he had something urgent to discuss with her. He was apprehensive over the phone. He needed her help, he said, and she'd asked him to come over to the house. He never told her he was coming with someone.

"He's not alone, Ma," Nick said.

"Tell him I will join him shortly." Jennifer turned to go into her room. She was wearing a nightgown, and now she needed to change to something else. She didn't know who it was that Pius had brought along with him.

She walked past the foyer, looking at herself and Chief in a frame hanging on the wall. The picture was taken at one of their business dinners. The wall of the mansion had paintings and similar images, taken at lavish events.

The mansion had five sitting rooms. Chief had built it as his palatial home, and spent recklessly on the furnishings and decor.

Jennifer, her son Junior, Nick, and sometimes Jennifer's Gozy when he visited, were the only people occupying the thirteen-bedroom mansion. Rita didn't stay much in the house since she returned from London. Not that Jennifer cared. Sometimes, she spent the night and was out very early, before anyone knew it. Jennifer suspected she could be up to something.

Jennifer had asked the housemaids and other domestic staff to move into the boys' quarters. She would call any of them when she needed them. She didn't want anyone snooping around the house. She didn't want anyone running into her when she was with Gozy.

Dressed in a less revealing cloth, with her hairnet on, she descended the stairs and went into the sitting room. A crowd of unfamiliar faces waited for her.

"Good evening, Madam," The group chorused.

"Good evening," Jennifer responded as she glanced at them, trying to hide her surprise at their presence in her house. "Barrister Pius, what's going on?" She wished she could scream at him.

"Madam, I have a problem. A big problem, but please can we step aside and talk?"

"No. Tell me who these people in my house are. I'm not sure I'm safe with this number of men in my house," she stated coolly.

"Madam, you are safe," Mr Solomon added as she drew closer from where he sat.

Jennifer looked closely at him.

"I know you. You work at Onu Group. Aren't you Mr Solomon?"

"Yes, Madam!"

"And that's Mr Sani, Mr Patrick…um, you work at the group?"

"Yes, and Mr Segun here also," Mr Solomon added as they all came together, separating themselves from the rest.

"So, what are you all doing in my house this night?"

"Madam, we…we—"

"Are you aware that my husband is dead and that I'm mourning?"

"Yes, Madam, we are aware. We are sorry for your loss and we feel it so terribly."

"Is that why you are here? The condolence register is outside."

"Um…um, not really, Ma. We were fired from our jobs and we thought…"

"You were sacked and you had to come to my house? Am I the Managing Director of the Group or is this house the company's headquarters?"

"Madam, please, can I have a moment you?" Pius asked.

Pius and Mrs Jennifer walked towards the staircase.

"Barrister, what is this?" She hissed angrily.

"Madam, please don't be angry. I have an issue with those men. I went to watch a football match and they held me hostage. They said they were dismissed, and I came to see how you could help. You are the only solution I have right now."

"That's why I told you not to go out without Nick and the driver."

"Madam, I'm sorry about that."

"I am aware that they were sacked. I'd spoken with the MD on their issue and I know they gave you money."

"Madam, you knew that?"

"Yes, Barrister. I knew they would come after you. That is why I asked the MD to relieve them of their jobs. I didn't want them interfering with you. But you see you have given them the exact opportunity I was avoiding."

"Please, Madam, help me. They've got me in a bad spot. They promised that if I'm able to talk to you to get them their jobs back, they will let me be."

"Are you sure about that?"

"Yes, Madam. I seem to not have any other options."

Jennifer thought about this for a while. She knew very well that she needed Pius for the tasks ahead and one way to be assured of his loyalty was to help him.

"Okay, I will do it," she said. "You understand the tasks ahead?"

"Yes, Madam. Thank you. Thank you very much."

Jennifer came back with Pius and informed Mr Solomon and the others that she'd spoken with Pius and that she understood their needs. She would put a call across to the MD to reinstate them.

They thanked her and left. Pius didn't leave with them.

CHAPTER 15

Morning mass had just ended. Emeka waited for the crowd to disperse before he went into the church. If he had tried to force himself through, they would have gotten in his way. There were so many parishioners that morning and they'd taken over all the doors leading into the church building. Each one of them hurried out to catch up with resumption at work. It was 7:24 a.m.

When the crowd had dispersed considerably, Emeka quietly walked into the church. It had a beautiful marble wall, bespoke wooden seats, captivating lightings and paintings of biblical events on the ceiling. It was a true reflection of heavenly beauty. He looked at the altar and it reminded him of the days when he was an altar boy.

He was suddenly disturbed by how distant he'd become with God. For several years he hadn't been to any church. Sundays had become the days he rested and played football. It wasn't always like that. He used to be a devout Catholic. He was one of those who said the Rosary every day and who wouldn't miss Mass for anything.

A Catholic priest had once said that man had a spirit, a soul, and a body. Even though a man could be alive, he could be dead if he allowed his spirit and soul to suffer death. *Was he dead, spiritually*, he wondered.

He passed the confession box and shook his head. He thought about the last time he confessed his sins to a priest. He couldn't even remember. He couldn't recollect the last time he took communion either.

...and when he had given thanks, he broke it and said, this is my body, which is for you; do this in remembrance of me.

"Oh Lord, please help me," he whispered, as the scripture got hold of him. "I'm so lost. Mother Mary, pray for me."

Emeka dropped to his knees and began praying. There were two women praying at the altar, but each was quietly speaking to God on their needs.

"Lord, help me to nurture forgiveness in my heart," he prayed. It was his greatest undoing, he thought. After Dogo had spoken to him the night before, he'd assured himself he would come before God and ask for help.

"Here I am, Lord. I am still your son. The one you sent your begotten Son to die for his sins. Lord, please help me to forgive my mother," he continued.

Thoughts of her troubled him. How was she? Where was she? Mr Tim had said she was the person who first informed Chief that he was his son. Was she truly concerned about him, or was she doing it for her own self-interest?

"Lord, forgive me, my mind keeps wandering. I know you are still here," he said. "Please help me find the strength to forgive my mother."

He opened his eyes and glanced sideways only to see that one of the women at the altar was looking at him. *Have I been shouting?* He wondered. He wouldn't blame himself; he was desperate for solutions and anyone in his shoes would do same. That was why it was often said that the he-goat in its desperation for solution to its body smell sniffs her mother's *punani* to find out if his body odour followed him from the mother's womb.

He looked again at the woman, but this time her eyes were closed as she shook her head and prayed. His eyes darted towards a big cross hanging at the altar, again reminding him of the life of an altar boy.

He realized how much he'd fallen apart with the things of God. How disconnected he had become from God. It began with him missing a service, and then he couldn't go because he thought he was busy and then gradually it became a norm.

And let us consider one another in order to stir love and good work, not forsaking the assembling of ourselves together...

In truth he couldn't deny the impact the sermons had on him when he went to church. He was also able to say his confessions, and this helped him find some peace over some hurt, such as the hurt he had felt about his mother.

Lord, what do I make of this new family? he thought. A child without a father figure is likened to an aged man without his walking stick. He must learn new ways to walk without falling. It was worse, however, where such child also lacks the nursing of a mother, and this was his lot as he continued to wonder what it was like to suddenly discover he had a father, a stepmother, and siblings. How many were they? Where were they? He still didn't know much about them and hadn't asked his lawyer.

Would they accept me? Again, he wondered, interrupted by another saying of his grandmother that monkeys know that no matter how pretentious plantain could be, it will never be same as banana. Would they really accept him as one of their own? Perhaps they would be angry at him, thinking he had come to cause a tussle over the wealth with them. But who wouldn't?

But it wasn't me. Chief came looking for me and not the other way, he thought. But then, Chief was dead. What was he like?

The little he knew about him were from stories he had heard from senior staff. Chief was strict, an astute businessman who didn't take any excuses. He'd never met him before. It dawned on him that he truly needed someone who knew Chief, and his mother was the only person he could think of.

How I wish I'd met him, he thought. How I wish we knew each other as father and son. How many times in the past he wished he knew who his father was.

Emeka's prayer time had become an opportunity for deep reflection. His mind danced around so many thoughts at the same time, each issue becoming a new prayer point. The coconut water is valued not because it quenches thirst but because of where it comes from. He drifted deeply into his thoughts only to be startled by the sound of his phone ringing.

"Hello," he answered, after it rang for the second time. He hurriedly said the grace, ending his prayer when the phone kept ringing repeatedly. "Hello, Barrister," he said into the mouthpiece of the small Nokia phone Tim had given him.

"Where are you, Emeka?"

"I'm in church. St Bede's Catholic Cathedral on Ironsi road."

"I'm coming to pick you now. We are going somewhere. Please come out to the gate of the church. I'm using an Uber so I can't keep the driver waiting."

"Okay, Barrister," Emeka said, and the call ended.

He got up, made the sign of the cross, and walked out of the church, leaving behind the two women praying.

***

"You are a spoilt brat," Jennifer started to speak, "a spoilt child whose behaviour worried Chief until his death. You broke his heart and he kept talking about you till he died." She continued to comb her hair.

"Look at who is talking," Rita retorted. "The same woman who never had time for my father. You think I didn't know about your acts?"

Rita was perched on the arm of a chair.

There were two of them, with Pius the third person in the sitting room. Since the last incident involving Mr Solomon, Jennifer had insisted on Pius spending the day in the house and to be taken to the hotel at night.

"I will slap you," Jennifer said as she dropped the brush and charged towards Rita.

"You dare not."

Rita moved away from the chair and folded her hands into fists.

"You think I'm the small girl you could throw around some years back. If you try it, I will deal with you," she threatened.

"Enough!" Pius shouted from where he sat. He got up and went to stand between the two ladies.

"Both of you need to take it easy. Chief is dead and wouldn't want this. At this time, both of you have to come together and plan the burial and—"

"We are not coming together for anything," Rita said, still charged for a fight. "We are going to—"

Jennifer picked up her brush and continued brushing her wig but didn't stop mumbling, her anger very evident. Rita sat down and continued to mumble as well. Had Pius not intervened, they would have fought. It was enough, for now, to mumble and curse each other. As this went on till, Musa, the gateman, ran into the sitting room panting.

"Madam! Madam, some people are at the gate. They said they want to see *Oga's* family," he said.

"Tell them I'm not seeing anyone now," Jennifer said and continued with the task before her.

"Madam, I told them that but they wouldn't leave. They've been at the gate for over thirty minutes."

"Open the gate," Jennifer said as she dropped the wig and brush and began to walk outside. "Who's that? We aren't in the mood for this now. Who are they? Bring them in. What do they want? Are they not aware that Chief is in the morgue?"

Musa opened the gate and Tim, Chris, and Emeka stepped into the compound. Emeka looked around, spotting the exotic cars parked nearby.

"Good afternoon, Madam. I'm Tim," he said. "And these are Emeka and Mr Chris."

"Yes, what do you want? I don't have time to waste."

Pius and Rita were watching what was going on. Rita had come to stand beside Jennifer.

"Madam, may we at least go inside and talk?" Chris said.

"Go inside where?" Jennifer interjected. "Who do you think you are to walk into my compound and be requesting to go inside? Say whatever you want to say here." She took a stern look at Rita standing beside her.

"Okay then. If you insist." Tim said. "We are here to speak with the family. We heard about Chief's death—"

"Speak with the family about what?" Jennifer asked.

"To let you know that Emeka here is Chief's son."

"What kind of stupid joke is this? Musa, how did you let this people into my compound? Get out!"

"They are not going anywhere. Did you say I have a brother? This guy here is my brother?" Rita asked.

"Yes," Tim responded quickly.

"Musa! Get these people out right now."

"Please make *una* leave. *Madam no want you people.* I don't want to lose my job *o*. Please leave!"

"Musa, they are not going anywhere," Rita interjected.

"Small Madam, you say *wetin*? Big madam, you say?"

"Could you at least tell us how you came to this conclusion?" Pius asked. Although unsure of what was happening, he felt it was important that he say something.

"They are not telling us anything. We can't hear or listen to this nonsense. Why didn't you say it when Chief was alive? He's dead and you are bringing this grown man as his son."

"Chief was aware!" Chris affirmed.

"Get out!"

Musa succeeded in getting them to leave for the sake of his job. As he led them outside the compound, Rita followed them.

CHAPTER 16

Rita picked up the last slice of the pizza. She had shared most of it with Jack. They were at his place, a two-bedroom apartment he'd just rented. Lately, she'd spent more time at his place, and they would often gist over pizza, shawarma or roasted yam.

"I gotta take a shower," she said and left for the bathroom.

"You mind if I join you?" Jack asked, pouring the last wine into a glass cup.

"If you wish," Rita responded and dropped her gown on the floor, leaving just her panties. Jack followed her movement with his eyes.

He poured the rest of the wine in the cup into his mouth, put out the cigarette in his hand, and stood up. He pulled down his boxers so he had nothing on.

Jack made sure the front door was locked before leaving the sitting room. The TV set and the sound system were still on.

"Is the water warm enough?" he asked.

"Not yet, the heater is on, though," Rita answered as she stood in the running shower.

Jack stepped in and held her waist. She turned, and their faces met.

"You sure you wanna shower or you want something else?" Rita asked as she rubbed her body against his.

"I want to shower."

"You sure you wanna shower?" Rita asked again, but this time she rubbed her wet hands on his chest, letting the running water drop.

"I...I... want to..." Jack made an effort to speak but couldn't because her lips were already against his.

"Let me spoil you." Rita whispered, as she loosened her grip of his lips. She bit his chest, touching his skin with her tongue as the running water flushed down his body.

"Oh Baby...you are going to kill me tonight," Jack said. He let her work on him while the water ran. She did work on him for a while and stopped.

"What happened, babe?"

"I can't seem to do this, you can't have me tonight," she said and walked out of the shower.

"You turn me on and let me off, what is this, babe?"

"Because I'm not in the mood. Please have your shower so I can come have mine."

"Something worries you?"

"Yes."

"What is it?"

"A lot isn't going right with our plans. I'm afraid I might lose everything. My stepmother has got the lawyer. She has control of the companies and just everything seems to be working in her favour."

"What do you want me to do?" Jack asked. He washed off the soap lather on his face so he could look at Rita.

"I want you to initiate the plans we had for her. I want her arrested," Rita said, playing with the soap pack in the sink.

"You mean I should release the video and evidence to the police?"

"Yes, you should do that now."

"I thought we were keeping that for later?"

"I can't seem to think of any better plans right now. I need her out of my way. If she's arrested and kept in custody, everything will fall back in place."

"Babe, you should consider that done. Do you want to come over now?"

"Did I tell you a guy came to say he's my father's son?"

"You said so. What about him?"

"I'm surprised how I missed that. If my father knew he was his son, it means he might will some things to him."

"Does the issue about the boy trouble you?"

"I'm not worried about him because I know there is no way my father will give all he has to him. I've tried to find out more about the boy. He doesn't seem like a bad person, and I think I can handle him."

"Had Jennifer tried getting close to him?"

"That's the thing. She doesn't seem to see him as anything. In fact, I'm glad she doesn't because I would have been worried if she had teamed up with the boy. The boy is quiet and naïve but the men leading him on aren't."

"That's a good sign then."

"Yes, I've made efforts to get close to the boy and he's been receptive. He wants a sister and I'm ready to give him that."

"I bet you are."

"But I'm worried about that witch. Something about her confidence worries me. She feels that she and her bastard son would inherit all my father's wealth and she's got the lawyer in her pocket."

"Have you tried speaking with the lawyer?" Jack was out of the shower and had picked up the towel to dry himself.

"I've tried but he wouldn't listen to me."

"What do you mean?"

"I've tried to talk to him about Jennifer but he wouldn't believe me and of recently I can't get any opportunity to speak with him because Jennifer's errand dog, Nick, is always with him."

"That fat idiot. Why not call him on the phone?"

"I've tried that also, but he wouldn't speak freely, and each time I called it was as if someone was listening to our conversation. He always says he would call back but he never does."

"Babe, you have to find a way to get through to him."

"You bet I will. I just don't have time, That's my problem. I suspect my father made a will and it's in his custody."

"Of course, your father should have a will," Jack said as he bent to pick his boxers.

"You didn't mention that to me. If you suspected so, why didn't you mention that?" Rita asked and walked into the room where Jack was wearing his boxers.

"But how would I have known you didn't know that?"

"That's what you have to say?"

"What do you want me to say?"

She sighed. "I don't blame you. I blame myself for not thinking it through. I can see why I need a lawyer in my life. If I had a lawyer, it would have been easier to see this coming."

"It's okay, babe."

"Don't tell me it is okay when it's not. How could we be smart about everything and leave out the most important thing? If, in our plans, we didn't think about the will, then we planned to fail."

"It's going to be fine," Jack said as he walked to hold Rita.

"You know it wouldn't be fine by just by saying it. Something has to be done for it to be fine."

"I will do something about it," Jack said as he kissed her on the neck.

"I wouldn't let things get out of hand," Rita said.

"Enough of the talk, let's have some moment." Jack kissed her and lifted her off her feet, her towel dropped on the floor.

CHAPTER 17

"Has Junior eaten?" Jennifer asked her maid in the kitchen.

"Yes, Madam," the maid responded.

"Junior, what did you eat?" she asked as she bent over her son busy with his building blocks by the dining table.

"Aunty Amaka gave me *jollof* rice," Junior answered. "Mommy, see, I'm building a house."

"That is good. Are you going to let your mommy live with you in the house?" Jennifer asked as she examined the blocks her son put together.

"Yes, Mom. I'm building it for you and Aunty Rita," the kid said and smiled.

"Aunty Rita?" Jennifer asked. She sat down and drew her son close.

"Yes, Mom. I want to build this for you and her since Daddy is dead. It means he won't come home again, right?"

"Daddy is resting. He won't come home," Jennifer said to her son, reassuring him that all would be fine. The boy looked at her, teary-eyed.

For a moment, his looks reminded her of his father, Gozy. Jennifer had spent a weekend with him, one of the many times when Chief travelled for business. She had missed her period but was sure to spend more time with Chief when he returned. Not long after, she broke the news to him that he was going to have a son.

That was just the news Chief wanted. He was happy, and he did everything she wanted afterwards. She gave birth in the United States of America.

The birth of Junior established her position with Chief. She became emboldened and would confront him on anything; after all, she was the mother to the heir to his wealth. If she had any regrets about the child, they faded away.

Something troubled her, though. When Junior was just a baby, Chief would come home early to spend time with him. He would cradle him, feed him, and do just about anything a father would do for his only son. He looked forward to those moments and wouldn't let anything disrupt those times.

With time, he began to change as Junior grew older. Perhaps as the boy looked less like him. He began to spend less time with him, though he would touch him and play with him on rare occasions.

Jennifer had confronted him about this but when he didn't budge, she let it go. It didn't matter after all, she thought. The child was legally his and there was nothing he could do about it.

"You will build the house for me but not Rita," she corrected as she patted his head.

"Mommy, why do you say that? I love Aunty Rita too."

"She doesn't love you. Going forward, you don't need to be with her anymore. She is not a good person."

"But Mommy, she buys me things and likes playing with me."

"She is not a good person Junior. You can't be seen taking anything from her. If you do and I find out, I will beat you."

"Sorry, Mommy."

"Okay, my boy. Just don't get Mommy angry, okay?"

"I will not."

"Amaka! Amaka!"

"Madam," Amaka responded as she ran out from the kitchen.

"Henceforth, do not let Rita give anything to my son. If she does, collect it and keep it for me. Have you heard me?"

"Yes, Madam."

"Any day you let my son eat anything or use anything from her without letting me know, that day you will cease working for me and I will make sure you are arrested by the police."

"Ah! Madam, I will not."

"Has Barrister Pius eaten something?"

"Yes, Madam. I took food to the room he stays in sometimes. When I asked, he said I should bring the food to the room."

"That's fine."

"Madam, Musa said someone is at the gate."

"Why couldn't he call me on the intercom and tell me himself?"

"He spoke to me through the kitchen window. I don't know why he refused to call."

Jennifer got up and went to the door.

"Musa! Musa!"

"Yes, Big Madam." Musa ran from his gate to the door where Jennifer stood looking at the gate.

"Who is at the gate?"

"Madam, he said he is a Barry Yusuf. I tell am make him wait make I ask permission."

"And did you come to ask for that?"

"No, Ma. I think say you busy, so I ask Amaka to help me check."

"Whatever. Open the gate. Who is this Barry?"

Musa opened the gate and a middle-aged man, dressed in black suit with a file, walked into the compound.

"You are Barry?" Jennifer asked the man approaching.

"No, Mrs Onu. I am Barrister Yusuf Umar. I guess he mistook the Barrister for Barry." The man smiled as he glanced at Musa and back to Jennifer.

"How may I help you, Mr Yusuf?" Jennifer asked.

"I am here in respect of a message from Chief."

"Which Chief? My husband?"

"Yes, Madam."

"Ah! *Oga don* message from the land of dead," Musa screamed and stepped away from the man.

"You are aware that he is dead?"

"Yes, Madam. I'm aware."

"You said he messaged you?" Jennifer asked again to be sure she'd heard correctly.

"Yes, Madam. He made a will which is in my custody. I wish to meet you and every member of his family to agree on a date to read the will."

"My husband made a will and you have custody of it?"

"Yes, Madam. It's secured in a safe."

"Get out of my house," she screamed. "What sort of nonsense is this?"

"Madam, won't you wait to listen to me?"

"There is nothing to listen to. Please get out."

Musa had run ahead to open the gate.

Mr Yusuf was hesitant to leave but noticing the woman was going to embarrass him, he turned and began to leave.

"Wait. What is your phone number and do you have an office?" Jennifer asked the man who had reached the gate.

"My number and address are on my card." He handed his complimentary card to Musa and left.

Musa locked the gate and ran to hand the card to Jennifer. She collected it, hissed and went back into the mansion.

CHAPTER 18

Gozy had just woken up, lighted his cigarette, and poured himself a glass of Champagne. He looked over the bed, and across the room, littered with women, blonde haired, light and dark-skinned, every one of them fast asleep.

Damn! He had had a busy night.

His phone rang. He ignored it the first time, but when it kept ringing, he lifted two bodies on him aside, stepped over them, and got up.

"It's Mama J calling." He had to take the call.

"Hello, Mama J," he spoke into the mouthpiece.

"Hun, where have you been? I've been calling you," Jennifer said on the other end.

"I was in the toilet. I came out not cleaning my butt," he lied.

"Gozy, that's not funny, go clean up yourself."

"I'm good. I already did," he said. One of the girls had stretched, opened her eyes, and was going to say something but Gozy quickly signalled to her to be silent.

He ran into the toilet, and turned the water closet knob, so it sounded as though he'd just flushed his poo.

"What is it, Mama J?" he asked.

"We have some trouble," she said. Her voice was shaky.

"Calm down, Mama. What is it?"

"A man came here a while ago claiming that Chief made a will and that he has possession of it."

"Did he look like he was bluffing?"

"He didn't, and in fact he dropped his complimentary card. I checked it out; his law firm is a known firm in town."

"That's serious."

"I'm worried. I don't want anyone to know about this. I want him to be dealt with."

"Killed, you mean?"

"Yes, of course. If he's dead, how will he present the will?"

"That's true. Has anyone else heard this?"

"It was him, me, and Musa, but I don't think Musa understood anything we discussed. Musa called the man Barry Yusuf, mistaking same for barrister. Musa is an *olodo*."

"The man's name is Yusuf?"

"Yes, Barrister Yusuf. His card says Yusuf Umar Esq. I haven't heard of him before but when I Googled it, I found out that he's a public interest lawyer."

"Don't worry, Mama. I will take care of him. I will come to the house to finalise plans with you."

"When are you coming? I miss you."

"I can come later today; however, my challenge is your lawyer you've kept in the house. I don't like him. I think we should meet at the hotel."

"Don't worry, you know he is only here for a while and you know sometimes he stays at the hotel."

"Mama, you need to let him leave sometimes. I can't come freely with him there."

"I agree. But for this we can meet and discuss at the hotel. I also need to spoil you."

"That's my sweetie," Gozy joked. "Honestly, when I saw your

call, I thought you were calling to inform me that you sent me money. I'm running out of cash."

"I gave you two million naira just last week. What are you doing with money?"

"You know I'm living in a hotel and I have other expenses."

"I'll see what I can do about that."

"That's my Mama J. You know I love you deeply. Come over and let me treat you well tonight."

"Leave me *jor*. That's what you say."

"See you," Gozy said and hung up. He would have to check out of the hotel and head to the Hilton where he had a reserved room and where he usually met with Jennifer. He quickly sat up and moved to the door.

As he turned the toilet knob, and opened the door, he saw that one of the girls was at the door.

"What are you doing?" he asked, surprised. *Had she been listening to my conversation*, he wondered.

"I want to use the toilet, but you were there for some time."

"You can use it. You girls need to leave because I'm checking out of this hotel now. I have an important meeting," he said.

"Whatever," the girl responded and entered the rest room.

* * *

Pius was reading *Shadows*, a book by Tony Ekwoaba, when he heard the knock on the door. He was on page 149, and not wanting to forget the page, he flipped it and dropped the book on the bed.

"Come in," he said.

Jennifer opened the door and quietly walked into the room.

"I hope I'm not disturbing your quiet time, Barrister?"

"No, I'm just reading a novel. Someone had mentioned it and

I picked it up. I didn't know the author but it's quite impressive. It's a Nigerian legal thriller."

"That's good. Do you have some time?"

"Of course, have a seat," Pius said, pointing to another chair in the room. He was sitting in front of a reading table.

"You still insist on not having a television or radio in this room?" Jennifer asked as she looked around the almost empty room. Aside from the bed, table, and two chairs, the room was empty.

"Yes, I insist. I want to be able to think. Those things will distract me and besides that, anytime I need those I will go to my hotel room. I will be going to the hotel today."

"If you insist then," Jennifer stated and sat down. "Amaka told me you've eaten."

"Yes, I have. Thank you."

"I have something troubling me and I wish to share it with you."

"What is it, Madam?"

"A man came to the house a while ago, saying that he is in custody of a will made by Chief. I didn't believe him, but I don't want to be ambushed."

"A will made by Chief?" Pius asked, surprised. "What then do you have?"

"I wonder what nonsense the man is saying. I don't want him going about saying that rubbish. I want to have him eliminated," Jennifer stated softly.

"I don't get it?"

"I will arrange to have him killed. If he's dead, he can't be saying that rubbish."

For a moment, Pius was confused about what response to give. The woman spoke innocently, yet very coldly. Pius wished she was joking, but a glance at her face convinced him that she meant what she said.

"Do you know the man?" Pius found himself asking.

"He left his card. He's a lawyer. It won't be difficult to track him. His name is Barrister Yusuf Umar," she responded.

"I don't think killing him will solve the problem," Pius stated, still amazed at what he was hearing.

"What do you mean? If he's dead, he will be unable to present any will."

"Because the copy he has might not be the only copy of the will. The will may also have been deposited somewhere."

"You mean it?"

"Does it mean the will you have isn't deposited at the probate registry?" Pius asked, wondering why he hadn't known this all along.

"What is that? The copy I have is the only copy I know of."

Pius thought about it for a while. If the will the woman had wasn't deposited anywhere, it pointed to one probable conclusion – the will the woman had been brandishing wasn't made by Chief Onu. And if it wasn't made by Chief Onu, that meant it was doctored. Chief couldn't have made his will without having a lawyer present. If he had a lawyer involved, it would have been deposited at the probate registry. He'd thought of this but didn't think Chief's wife would doctor her late husband's will.

He had to act fast, he thought. If this woman could dare to take a life for the will, a lawyer's for that matter, it meant everything wasn't the way it seemed. It was clear he wasn't safe with her.

"Don't worry, that copy you have is okay," Pius said, trying to sound as believable as he could.

"If you say so, Barrister. What do you say about taking the stupid man down?"

"I don't think it's necessary. I will let you do that if I see need for that. I don't think he is a threat yet," he lied.

"If you say so, Barrister." She said and wondered if she had said so much to Pius. She waved off the thought of his betrayal and concluded that if he gave any sign of that she would have him killed. "I will leave you to continue with your reading." Jennifer forced a smile.

"Thank you. I should be leaving for the hotel much later."

"That's fine. I will ask the driver to drop you."

"Thank you, Madam," Pius said and picked the book.

Jennifer took a final glance around and left the room.

CHAPTER 19

Dorothy Okoromadu received the news from her brother as a miracle. Her lost son had reached out, saying he would like to meet with her, and it was urgent. Her brother had said he was in Abuja. It meant she would have to book a direct flight from Nairobi to Abuja immediately.

Emeka hadn't really been missing, but he had refused to maintain any form of communication with her. *It wasn't his fault,* she thought. She had abandoned the boy for far too long, leaving her mother to train him. Since her mother died, she had paid no attention to him, but could you really put the blame on her? Life hadn't been fair to her either. She had been pregnant with him when she couldn't even take care of herself as a girl.

She worked as a call girl in Lagos. One evening, a young man had come into her room for her services. After they negotiated her terms and she received her pay—she always insisted on it before her services—the young man told her it was his boss that requested her service. She was infuriated but later gave in. It was done in haste. He'd said something about losing his wife and was in pain. He apologized. It was perhaps his first time with a call girl. He paid her extra and sneaked out. That was the last she saw of him.

Not long after the encounter, she started feeling feverish. She knew he used protection, but then it had punctured, and she only noticed this when she went to dispose of it. It was one of the very rare occasions she was been careless. The fever persisted; she took several tests that came out negative. Someone had suggested she take a pregnancy test and she refused, dismissing the idea. One month after, she learnt that she was pregnant.

She had thought of having an abortion but couldn't go through with it. Of course, keeping the baby came with a price. She couldn't do her job because she was no longer attractive to customers. Men who insisted on sex with pregnant women were known to do so for ritual purposes. The girls who dared do so for the enticing sum they offered usually died shortly after or lost their babies. When she couldn't afford to pay her rent, the owner of the brothel asked her to leave. She was stranded and couldn't think of anywhere else to go other than the village. She returned to her mother, pregnant.

Her mother wasn't welcoming at all. She punished her for her mistake. Each day, she reminded her that while her mates brought home husbands, she'd brought a pregnancy out of wed-lock. She woke up each day to those hurtful words and she swore that once she delivered the child, she would leave the child with her and go reclaim her life.

Her plan was to go back to Lagos, or any other city in Nigeria. While she worked on her plan, she hoped for something better, so she could avoid the pains of Lagos. When an opportunity came for a trip to Ghana, she took it. She lived in Ghana for some years, working as a hotel cleaner, before moving to Nairobi.

Donald said Emeka told him it was urgent, she thought. "What was wrong that he suddenly wanted to see me? I hope he's fine. I hope my baby is fine," she muttered.

Her love for him grew with each day that passed and she

would often wonder whether it was a mother's warmth for her child or because she'd found out the man who got her pregnant was a wealthy man. Whichever it was, she couldn't say. She knew she'd missed him dearly and had realized her need for a child. Unmarried, uneducated, yet tied to a seven-to-six job as a cleaner in an accounting firm in Nairobi with no child. Nothing was more unsettling than waking up each morning to these realities, and the mounting fear of what would become of her as old age approached.

She'd been planning her return since she received the call. Her stay in Nairobi hadn't really earned her much. She barely survived and had nothing to brag about the years she spent in the country. She'd managed to get him some shirts. She wasn't sure of his size nor his height, but she'd come up with something using a picture of him that Donald had sent on WhatsApp – a handsome young man. The same picture she sent to Chief, informing him that he had a son. She'd got a medium size, hoping it would fit. She couldn't walk up to him empty-handed.

She'd been battling whether or not to prepare herself as someone who was leaving not to come back. It was a tough call, but she had to make it. She had to find a way to convince herself that she was going to settle in Nigeria. There were concerns of insecurity, but she promised herself she would find a way to survive. It was her first trip to Nigeria since she left Ghana. The flight tickets were expensive, and she didn't have any reason to trouble herself about home. Her mother was dead, not that she would say they were on good terms. But now the urge was there, to see her son again.

"Oh my little boy," she said, recalling her memories from when he was a baby.

Another angle to it was that she needed to sort out the issue with the man who had impregnated her. It was a miracle that the boy requested she come home because she'd been looking for how to find him and break the news to him. He used to be in contact with Donald, but for the past few years Donald said he hadn't called and the number he was using was no longer available. It was a dream come true, she thought, because she couldn't have established her claim about the child if the child couldn't be found.

Her flight was an Ethiopian flight ET 309. She had to sell most of her things to raise her flight ticket fare. She'd asked her boss for leave to travel. She was needed urgently in her country, she said. Fortunately, he'd granted her request and wished her a safe trip. When he asked when she would be back, she'd told him within a month. She knew she wouldn't return to Kenya for anything, though her spirit had led her to not resign because of the uncertainties ahead.

"Enjoy your stay and come back soon," two of her friends who saw her off to the Jomo Kenyatta International Airport said.

"Before you know it, I will be back," she said and waved goodbye. They were too trusting. She wondered why they didn't suspect she was gone for good when she sold most of her things and gave the rest away.

***

The ET 309 Boeing 737-800, Ethiopian flight touched down at 12:23 p.m.

Dorothy knew Emeka, Donald, and whoever else was with them would be waiting at the arrival wing of the Nnamdi Azikiwe International Airport. It had been agreed Donald and Emeka would come to the airport to pick her up. She'd sent them her flight itinerary.

She got off the plane and took a deep breath. The air, and every other thing, was different.

It didn't take long to get through Customs and while she was waiting to pick up the bag she'd checked, she sent Donald a message that she had arrived.

"See you soon," he replied. "We are waiting at the arrival lounge. You will see us once you step out."

* * *

Chris, Tim, Emeka, and Donald had been waiting at the arrival wing for over an hour. They had seen when the plane landed and had waited another thirty minutes before Donald received the message that she'd arrived. They were standing outside, because the airport security wouldn't let them in.

For most of the time they'd spent waiting, Tim narrated his travel experiences to the rest who hadn't travelled abroad before. He related his encounters in each airport he'd visited – Heathrow, Frankfurt, Hartsfield-Jackson. In one of the instances in London, he'd forgotten to buy an Oyster card at Heathrow and had followed someone through the barriers without paying and jumped in the bus. He thought he was smart, as no one was looking. He wouldn't be paying the bus ticket, but as he sat down in the bus, an inspector who'd noticed he didn't use the card had walked up to him and demanded he pay the fine of twenty-five pounds. The cost of the trip would have been two pounds. It was one of those things you experience in a country where the systems worked.

Chris and Donald paid attention to the stories, but Emeka was unsettled. His focus was on the flood of people that poured out of the flight that just landed, the same flight as his mother. The airport taxi drivers wouldn't let them be.

He'd seen a couple of persons he thought were his mother

but then he'd looked at the photo she'd sent through Donald and realized he was wrong. He kept looking out for her.

He was nervous. He wasn't sure how he would feel about her. It was true he'd prayed about it and forgiven her. It was true he'd put all the pain behind her, but he was uncertain how he would react, for someone he hadn't seen since he was a baby.

Would he hug her? Would he run after her and hold her? How would she feel about him? He wasn't sure about that either. He wondered what would happen.

Donald was the first to see her.

"There she is," he announced, and everyone turned.

Dorothy was tall, and walked elegantly, her luggage trailing her. She was rather lanky and wore a shirt and trouser. You would think she was in her twenties. She had removed her sweater and tied it around her waist, because the weather was warm.

"Wow. Thank God," they all intoned and walked briskly towards her.

Emeka was the first to get to her. She'd dropped her luggage and ran the fastest she could toward them, stretching her arms wide.

It was a hug that both son and mother had looked forward to.

CHAPTER 20

Pius had been restless since his last meeting with Jennifer. It had exposed the fact that there was some conspiracy he wasn't aware of. Something about Chief's will that he couldn't comprehend. He had to find out; it might just be his saving grace.

He knew it. Something wasn't right all along. Jennifer wasn't someone who would spend so much to bring him from Lagos to Abuja, pay his hotel bills and all other expenses for no reason. She even reinstated Solomon and the other employees who were sacked at his request.

He had always known some things didn't add up, but he had thought they were minor issues, such as that between Jennifer and her stepdaughter. He had never suspected it was so deep that she could doctor her husband's will.

His problem just got bigger, he thought, as he sat on the bed in his hotel room, his eyes staring blankly at the wall.

If Jennifer had no qualms about destroying a lawyer, it meant he wasn't safe either. She could take him down anytime.

He looked around the room. Perhaps there could be some recording device somewhere through which they would be listening to him now. He got up and searched the entire room, first checking the wardrobe where his clothes were kept, and then the bed, under the bed, the lamp, the phone. Nothing seemed suspicious or out of place. Still, the room didn't feel safe.

He sighed. If only he had money, he wouldn't have been this handicapped. Should he return to Lagos? Abandon everything and run before it was too late? But he couldn't do that because they knew too much. Nick already said it and it wouldn't be difficult to find him.

If only he had enough money to clear his debts, then he could live a normal life and not as a fugitive. He could rent a place.

He was Payilo! He was not running anywhere. He would face this problem head on.

He walked to the bed, picked the telephone, and rang the reception desk.

"Hello."

"This is Reception! Good afternoon, sir. How may we help you?"

"Please send someone to my room. I need to change my room."

"Is something wrong with the room?"

"I just want to change the room," he said and hung up.

As he dropped the phone, his iPhone rang. It was Thara calling.

At first, he left the phone to ring. He wasn't sure he wanted to speak with her at this time, but she wouldn't stop calling.

"Hello, Thara," he answered the call.

"Hello, smart man. Where are you?"

"In Abuja, of course."

"*Godiya ga Allah.* I'm coming over to the hotel. I'm close."

"You are what?" Before he could say anything further, she'd dropped the call.

***

Pius was with the hotel staff manager when he heard the knock on the door.

"You see what I'm telling you?" he said to the manager. "Everyone seems to know about this room."

He walked to the door and waited. There was another rap on the door.

"Who is that?" he asked.

"Thara."

He opened the door.

"Thara, when did you get back in town?" he asked and moved aside for her to come in.

"I came back yesterday," she said and dropped her phone and bag on the bed. She looked at the room and the manager who'd been nervous since she came in.

"The room looks the same," she said.

"What do you expect, it's a hotel room, not my personal apartment."

"Okay, sir, I will come back when you are free," the manager said and made for the door.

"Get me a room as soon as possible and get someone to move my things."

"Okay, sir," he said and walked out of the room.

"You are moving?" Thara asked.

"Yes."

"*Me ya sa*? You don't like the room?"

"I feel I've stayed in this room for too long. I want to feel another place," he lied.

"Okay then. I want to take my bath, I hope you don't mind?" She was taking off her clothes.

"Why would you just show up here without notice, Thara?" Pius asked, following her movements with his eyes.

"Because I missed you and you were on my mind while I was away," she said, looking at him.

"You mean that? How did the family matter you went to Kano for go?"

"It was great. My uncle wants to buy a property and he wants me to handle the transaction."

"Really?"

"Yes. He thinks I'm a good lawyer. Actually, I'd started a diploma in law at ABU Zaria but couldn't continue. My people still call me De Law."

"I didn't know that."

"Because I didn't tell you."

"Are you going to be the one to find the property for him?"

"They already found the property and have concluded a search. Now here is how I want you to come in. I will give you N30 million if you prepare the conveyancing documents."

Pius was silent. It was such news that made one dumb. One mystery about the legal profession was that a lawyer could be poor one moment and stupendously wealthy the next moment. A transaction could change everything. It was about his network and his ability to deliver on time. Sometimes the people you least expected brought the briefs – a boy with an aunty abroad, a guard that overheard a discussion, a driver who had earned the trust of his boss.

"How quickly do they want this?"

"Like right now. Why do you ask? Aren't you prepared to do it?" Thara probed, over the sound of the shower.

"I am prepared. In fact, I can get it ready right away," he responded. He knew he didn't have a laptop with him but one thing he'd learnt was to make his templates ready anywhere he went. Luckily, he had brought his NBA seal from Lagos. He would walk over to the business centre in the hotel, access his email where he had saved some precedents, work on it to suit the new transaction. These things may seem simple, but the truth is that a lawyer's skills were usually required to draft the best clauses that will meet his client's interest. After amendment, he would append his seal on it.

Pius remained seated on the bed, still dazed about what was going on. Thara's phone beeped. Pius looked at it. A WhatsApp message had just come in. He made to call Thara's attention to it, but then stopped when he saw the sender.

"Love Alhaji." And the message read, "Thara get the agreement. Meet me at my guest house. Am in Abuja tomorrow."

Pius didn't bother opening it. She would know if he did. He just knew what was going on. Alhaji wasn't any uncle to Thara, he was her Sugar Daddy and he had asked her to prepare the agreement so she could make money from it.

"What sort of property is it?" Pius asked, as he stood up and stepped away from the phone.

"It's a petrol station," she responded. She'd finished her bath and was drying herself with a towel she got from the bathroom.

"How much is the purchase price?"

"It's about a billion."

"And you want to give me thirty million naira, Thara?" Pius asked, remembering the Rules of Professional Conduct for lawyers. The girl was on track to make huge money from the transaction and give him peanuts.

"That's a lot of money still," she said. She'd stepped out of the bathroom in her underwear. "Do you know what it took me to convince my uncle to give me this deal and how many people are on him to get it?"

"I wouldn't want to know," Pius replied sarcastically.

"Then you take what I'm offering you or I can go somewhere else. You know I care about you, that's why I want you to do this."

"You are aware I will prepare Deed of Assignment, Sale Agreement, and Power of Attorney? Three documents and not just one."

"*Me yasa ba*. Isn't that why I'm paying you?" she asked as she put on her clothes.

Pius went over to her and kissed her.

"I know you aren't going to be getting anything less than a hundred million," he said, looking into her eyes. "It might be more, but I don't want to know. Let us do it by the ten percent, you give me fifty million of that and I will be fine. I really need this money, Thara," He almost pleaded.

Thara looked at him for a while, uncertain what to tell him. He grabbed her hands, as if to squeeze the answer out of her.

"Okay! Get it ready. My uncle wants it immediately," she said.

Pius kissed her, and she kissed back. He lifted her and dropped her on the bed. He'd lost interest after sleeping with her. One of the issues he had with women he'd been with, most of them were rigid and unadventurous, but this moment he didn't care anymore. He jumped in the bed.

CHAPTER 21

Everyone settled for Hungry Man restaurant, or rather, the majority did. For the past few minutes, driving from the airport, there had been some debate over where to go. Dorothy had said she wanted a taste of Nigerian-made delicacy before anything. She'd yearned for it and wouldn't really believe she was home yet until she had something local.

She had been screaming "Mr Biggs" only to be disappointed when she was told the franchise had shut most of its outlets. Emeka had asked what kind of food she wanted and she had said local Nigerian cuisine. That was when the arguments started.

Tim had suggested they go to Drumstick, Emeka interrupted with Jevenik, Chris insisted Niger Delta Restaurant was the best place for her. It wasn't just the place but the meal that mattered – Fisherman's soup, he said.

"What's that?" Dorothy asked, already salivating with the sound of that. "It sounds like something that has so much seafood."

"Trust me. You will be so glad you did."

It took another fifteen minutes from the City Gate to the City Park where the restaurant was.

"Nigeria hasn't changed much," Dorothy said as she looked

out through the window. She sat in the rear with Emeka and Donald. Tim was in front and Chris drove.

"How do you mean? How long have you been away, and do you mean there are no new structures and buildings?" Tim asked.

"I don't mean that. I can see some new roads, other infrastructures. I mean in terms of the lives of the people. They still sell things in traffic. I can see these boys running over to clean the car windscreens."

"Certain things are so peculiar about our people," Donald said. "Our people can't change from it."

"Truly, and it makes home so different."

"You don't find people hawking on the roads in Kenya?"

"You don't, and the place is very neat. It's a crime to be caught throwing dirt on the road."

"Really?" Tim asked.

"Yes, I read about that," Chris added. "Kenya is one of the countries I haven't visited and I long to visit there soon."

"Nairobi is great," Dorothy said. "But I must add, Abuja isn't a bad place also. It is a clean city and the roads are wide. I like what I see."

Chris parked right in front of the restaurant. Everyone came out of the car and went into the Hungry Man building, with Chris leading. It was just some minutes over 1 p.m. The place was yet to experience the rush hour.

They took a table; extra chairs were added so they could all be at the same table.

"Do you have Fisherman's soup?" Chris asked a young waiter who had brought the menu.

"Yes, sir."

"Bring me Fisherman's soup," Chris said. The rest followed suit.

Not long after, the big bowls of soup with little wraps of Semovita were served.

"This really looks and tastes good," Dorothy said immediately she took the first bite.

"Yes it is," Chris responded proudly.

"The soup is rich and much is in it also. The balls of Semovita only come as an extra bite," Donald stated.

"Yes. Yes," Chris responded, as he licked off the soup on his finger.

The next few minutes, every one of them took time to get enough of the meal. It took a while before anyone said anything. But when they had all had their fill, they spent the next moments talking about Chief and his investments. And because they were the only ones in that section of the restaurant, it was a good moment to talk over the meal.

***

As Rita was searching through the food rails for something to buy, she would try her hands at making something, her phone buzzed in her bag. She brought it out. It was Sharon calling.

"Hello, Sharon."

"Rita, your mama's gigolo is a dog," she said.

"Don't call her my mama. Stupid girl, what happened?"

"I can barely hear you, is someone with you?"

"I'm at Shoprite and I don't want to speak out loud, I don't want to take chances."

"Should I call back?"

"No, Sharon. Tell me what happened?"

"He's a dog. Can you imagine the guy had three of us and still wanted more? I am so tired, all the other girls are drained."

"That's what he is using to hold the foolish woman," Rita said. "So anything? Did you get anything from him?"

"Don't you trust your girl? He received a call. The way he panicked and rushed to take the call, I knew she was the caller."

"Did you hear what they discussed?"

"The idiot lied to her. Your stepmother can be so stupid."

"I know that. She has no problem trusting people. She thinks the boy is all hers."

"The boy is for *community service*. I don't think that guy goes to bed without a woman. He's a pig."

"Any useful information from the call?" Rita asked impatiently, uninterested in Gozy's lifestyle. It was stale news.

"Rita, I think they are planning to take someone down. I think she told him someone brought a new will. I don't know who but they want to kill the person. She is serious about that."

"You didn't hear who it was?"

"No. He was in the toilet and I was at the door. I could only make out the conversation from his own responses." Sharon continued, "I think they are meeting again, in some hotel I wouldn't know."

"It's at the Hilton. They have a permanent suite at the Hilton."

"That boy is really having fun. The woman is spending so much on him and he's flaunting money as though he's got a printing machine."

"Sharon, can't you see he's got a printing machine? That's how they have been burning through my father's hard-earned money."

"Truly, I know this can be painful."

"I hope he gave you some of it?"

"He gave us some cash and promised to meet us again. The fool thinks he's going to see my nakedness a second time. You know he's not my kind of client? I did this for you."

"I understand, girl. I gotta pay you for it."

"No problem. You do your thing."

"Sharon. I gotta go. Thanks a lot, darling."

She ended the call.

CHAPTER 22

The second call Rita received at Shoprite was also unexpected. She had put the items she wanted in the shopping cart and was in line to check out when her phone rang. She brought it out of her bag to see who was calling. She had made up her mind to return the call later. It was nearly her turn on the queue and she needed to catch up with Jack who'd been waiting in the car park. But when she saw who the caller was, she freaked out.

Dropping the cart with its content on the floor, she ran towards the aisle.

"Hello, Barrister Pius," she said, trying to sound formal.

"Hi, Rita. I'm sorry I missed your calls and messages."

"It's okay, sir," Rita replied, wondering why he eventually felt the need to call. It crossed her mind that Sharon had said Jennifer said someone had found a new will. Could it be Pius?

"I've been busy and unable to return your calls," Pius lied. For many reasons he wasn't ready to have any talks with Rita. But since the last encounter with Jennifer, he'd come to suspect the woman was as dangerous as Rita had said and maybe, even worse. He would like to know more.

"I understand, sir."

"I would like to make it up to you. Can we go out for lunch, so I make it up to you?" Pius smiled, expecting her response.

"That will be amazing," Rita responded. "Where do we meet? Your hotel room?"

"Somewhere different. I will text you the address. Meanwhile, I've changed my room. I'm now in room two-eighteen, in case you want to visit."

"Copy that."

"See you in the afternoon, then," Pius said.

* * *

Rita's lunch with Pius was at Grand Cubana Hotel, Jabi District. It was the second time they were going to meet, with each having some sort of expectation of the other. Pius knew he needed her, and of course Rita couldn't have wanted any lawyer but one that knew her family so well.

What was supposed to be a business meeting turned into a date. They talked about many things, including her father and her childhood. Rita had been laughing all along.

For some reason, Pius was relaxed around Rita, and she noticed this. When she asked, he said it was because he wasn't as tensed as he used to be. He was right, and he looked it. The deal with Thara had paid off well and she had given him the first tranche of the money, about thirty million naira.

"You look and smell different," Rita said as she eyed his Rolex Submariner.

"Yes, I do," Pius smiled and picked at the last slice of the first course.

A waiter stopped to clear the table. They sat in silence until he finished and left.

"I actually made some money during the week," Pius began,

thinking Rita may be wondering where he got all the money. He wouldn't want her to get any funny ideas.

"Really, people still make money like that?" Rita responded, not sure what else to say, even though she had no reason to not believe him.

"Of course. I am telling you because I do not want you to think that your stepmother may have given me this money."

"I wouldn't have thought so because I know she isn't that generous. Except for the one warming her bed. And I know that isn't you."

"How are you so sure about that?" Pius asked, smiling.

"Because I know her gigolo. I know you may have seen him also."

"That woman is a hard nut to crack," Pius said as he rubbed his hand over his head.

"She is crazy. I thought I told you that."

"Yes, you did."

"Why didn't you believe me then? Why do you seem to want to listen to me now?"

"The truth is that she told me that someone brought a new will. I never suspected that there was another will; from the way she said it, I began to think there is a lot going on that I need to know. Do you know about the will?"

"I don't. But what I believe is that any will she has is forged."

"I didn't think so until she talked about the other will. My fear is that she wants to get rid of the person."

"I told you, but you wouldn't believe me."

"Sincerely, I am sorry for doubting you, Rita."

"I do not hold it against you, Pius. I know you considered me a little girl."

The waiter came again, this time with the entrée. Rita kept quiet and watched him drop the food on the table.

"You mean, we are good?" Pius smiled and continued when the waiter left.

"Of course, we are good," Rita responded. "Or how else do I prove that? I can kiss you on the cheek to show you I have nothing on my mind." She didn't wait for his response but stood up and bent over the table, Pius had to do the same. But instead of kissing him on the cheek as she had said, she kissed him on the lips and lingered.

Suddenly, Rita broke the spell.

"What did I just do? What if someone was watching us?"

"No one would be watching." Pius smiled. "I paid for the private space, so we could have some privacy."

"You did what?" Rita asked.

"I paid so no one else could come in here while we are here," Pius said proudly.

He was so happy that he was gaining his confidence back. Since he received part of the money from Thara, he'd paid off some debts owed to Mr Solomon and the rest, bought some clothes and shoes and a wristwatch. Changing his hotel room had been a wise decision.

"You know how to make a spectacle of opulence. I've been wondering why no one has walked into this place since we came in."

"That's why. I knew you would find out. One thing I love about you is that you are smart, very smart, and wild at the same time."

"You think I'm smart?" Rita smiled. She was beginning to experience the Pius she desired, and she couldn't stop grinning from ear to ear.

"You are smart and wild. I love your wild side a lot." He was correct. He was yet to see any girl as wild as Rita and this had drawn him to her. He had been handicapped, knowing fully well that even if he wanted her in his life, he didn't have money to take care of anything. He'd depended on Jennifer and it was foolish to spend Jennifer's money on her. It had dampened his ego and any interest whatsoever he'd had in her. But since he got some money from Thara and there was more to come, he knew very well he could do anything he wanted.

"Pius, you need to stop looking at me like a child."

"Come here," Pius said, spreading his arms.

As Rita stood up, her short skirt made a good show of her legs. She walked over to sit on Pius' lap.

"Take your eyes away," she said as she noticed Pius couldn't stop looking at her legs.

"How could I stop beholding this beauty," he said, kissing her once again.

"Please promise you will help me get my father's wealth back. I need you to fight that mad woman."

"I can see that she is evil. I don't think your dad would like what she is doing. I don't only owe you that, I think I owe that to your father also," Pius said, and he meant it.

"For your information, I have arranged to release evidence I have against her to the police. In due time, they will arrest her for the murder of my father."

"That's good to hear." Pius stared at Rita, unable to take his focus away.

"Why are you looking at me like that?"

"I can't believe what an idiot I've been. To believe I neglected your company is unthinkable. I should spend more time with you Rita. I should spoil you. If you don't mind."

"I don't mind," Rita said and smiled. Things were working so fast and it felt as if she was dreaming. "What is your love language?"

"Love what?" Pius responded, spilling some food in his mouth. "Does love have its own language?"

"There are five love languages, which are acts of service, physical touch, spending quality time, receiving gifts, and words of affirmation. Which of them are top on your list?"

"What is yours?"

"You tell me yours first."

"I really don't know what it means, so I can't tell you mine, except you explain further."

"Love language is what someone in a relationship would expect from his partner. It's important for one to know what his partner likes. Many people make the mistake of trying to do what they like without considering what their partner likes. I want to know you better, that's why I'm asking. For me, top on my list of love language is receiving gifts and words of affirmation."

"Okay then. Good to know that. Mine would be acts of service and maybe physical touch."

"I bet you like that." Rita smiled.

"I'm glad you like gifts. I should take you out shopping then. Let me use the gents. I will be right back. Don't bother about the bill. I already paid when I booked."

"Okay."

Pius got up and went to the gents.

CHAPTER 23

Jack was scared that Rita might be in some kind of trouble. She hadn't come home for several days and she had refused to take his calls or respond to his messages. He assumed he would go to her father's house, and if she wasn't there, he would report her disappearance to the police.

He was contemplating how to pay a visit to her father's house. Rita had warned him already not to go there for anything. She said it was better for their relationship to remain a secret until they actualize their plan. It would curtail unnecessary exposure, she said.

Earlier on, he had disagreed with her on this, because he knew that oftentimes, relationships where parties were ashamed and unwilling to introduce each other to friends and family failed sooner rather than later. It was more of a *situationship* than a relationship. He was afraid theirs would end that way. But then, he saw sense in what she said. She was right. So long as she would let him meet her friends and family once they got over the issues before them, there really was nothing to worry about.

Being exposed to Rita's family meant an eye watching over him, including the evil gaze of Jennifer and her henchmen. This would restrict him from doing the things he did for Rita.

He resolved that should he not hear from Rita by the end of the day, he would go over to their house pretending he had worked for Chief some years ago and had stopped by to greet him since he was in the neighbourhood. He knew he would be told Chief was dead. He would express shock and ask about his family, including his daughter who he would have loved to console with before leaving.

He had it all worked out and he had played the questions over and over in his head in case he ran into Jennifer first and she decided to inquire further into who he was. He would be ready for her.

In the middle of all these thoughts, his phone rang. Thank goodness it was Rita calling.

"Babe, you got me anxious," Jack said as he quickly picked the phone on the table in his sitting room. "I thought something had happened to you."

"I'm fine, Jack," Rita responded.

"What is the matter? You haven't been taking my calls nor responding to my messages," Jack said, troubled that something wasn't right. She didn't call him Jack often and only did if she was incensed.

"Because I want to be left alone. Why do you keep calling? If someone doesn't take your call, shouldn't you know it's obvious she wants to be left alone?"

"Babe, what is going on?"

"Nothing is going on. I just want to be left alone and don't bother going to my house. I'm not there."

"Where are you? I want to come over and meet you now."

"Jack, I'm done with you. I need a break," she said and hung up.

"You need what? Rita! Rita!" Jack screamed but the line was dead.

He looked at the phone, wondering if it was a nightmare. But it was her voice and her phone and exactly the way she spoke.

"What is going on?" Jack asked. What game was she playing? He hadn't seen or heard her act like this before, not towards him.

Was that a breakup? Was Rita breaking up with him, just like that? Was she going to jettison the moments they had spent together? What about the things he was doing for her? He had made sacrifices trying to do lots of shady jobs for her and, in fact, there were some things he needed to discuss with her regarding their plans against Jennifer. Jack had a lot running through his mind at once.

"No! She won't be that stupid," he thought, "Not when I have the key to her means of bringing Jennifer down. She can't lay me off like that. After she agreed on what to give me for all my stress when she gets her money?"

"No! She was only joking. Maybe she's playing some sort of game." Jack got up from his seat in the sitting room and went to the room. He went over to the wardrobe where Rita kept her things.

"But her clothes are still here," he said to himself. "If she was running away, she would have taken them with her. She's coming back. My babe is playing," he said and smiled.

He turned to go back to the sitting room. But then, as if something struck him, he paused mid-stride.

"Rita is highly unpredictable. She's crazy in the head. Wait! This girl can do without all these things," he muttered. What if she was gone for good? What if she left the things to make him think she was coming back?

"There is only one way to find out," he said. "I have to check the place where I kept all the evidence against Jennifer."

He ran to his box where he kept the evidence, quickly opened it, searching for the photos and the tape.

They were gone!

* * *

Jennifer stood outside holding a glass of Champagne. She noticed the figure walking towards her and turned in its direction. It was Chief's younger brother who was a priest.

"Oh, Father Vitus! Welcome," Jennifer said, setting the glass on the side stool.

"Are you drinking?"

"Father, I've been crying all day. I came out here to have a drink, hoping it will help," she lied.

"I've been away on mission work and you couldn't even call me to tell me he was dead, Jennifer," he said as he went over to where a picture of Chief and the condolence register were kept.

"Father, I tried but I was told you were not in the country."

"Does it mean I can't be reached anymore? I'm on Facebook, I'm on Twitter and Instagram, and when I tried reaching you on those platforms all the messages I sent weren't replied to," he grumbled. "Anyway, that isn't a problem for me. You were not compelled to tell me."

"I'm sorry, Father."

"What plans have been made towards his burial? I'm back now and I want my brother laid to rest as soon as possible."

"You know Chief belonged to a lot of clubs and organizations. I am yet to reach a consensus with them on a date for the burial."

"You mean the clubs and organizations will decide the date for his burial, or you decide and communicate to them?"

"I don't know."

"My brother was a devout Catholic until he died, and I want him to be buried by the church. No one can deprive him of that and as you already know, the Catholic Church has a time within which a practicing Catholic must be buried. That timeframe has already been exceeded. Have you informed the village?"

"Some elders came here some days ago from the village."

"You haven't gone home or sent a delegation to the village?"

"Not yet, Father. We are yet to sort some things out here."

"Sort out things like what?"

"His will."

"What is that? You will wait until you share my brother's properties before we bury him?"

"Father, he made a will. I have the will."

"Whatever the case, I want this issue settled. Whatever you want to do, do it quickly. I don't care whether there is a will or not. I want my brother to be laid to rest soon."

"Yes, Father, soon we shall get over it."

"How are Junior and Rita?"

"They are fine. Junior is inside sleeping, but Rita is not in the house at the moment."

"Tell her I came. I need to see his body. Which morgue is he in?"

"He is in the Central Hospital Morgue. Do you have what you need to gain access to see him?"

"Don't worry, I will talk to them."

"I don't think you can see him without the tag. I gave them strict instructions on that," she stated. "Let me bring something that could help."

"Okay. I will wait."

Jennifer walked away as Father Vitus looked over the compound, he suddenly lost interest to go inside the mansion, his eyes momentarily resting on the mansion, cars, and the picture of his elder brother placed on the wall.

"*Nwoke Ike ala*! Indeed, all is vanity," he said, tears dripping from his eyes.

Jennifer returned with a card, and she handed it over to him. He thanked her, stood up and made for the gate.

"Call everyone together for a meeting. I want to be there also," he said before greeting Musa and exiting the compound.

"I will, Father." Jennifer responded.

CHAPTER 24

Jennifer paced in the dining room, her hair hanging loose, with the hassled look of someone who'd bumped into many enemies but didn't know who to begin a fight with. Rita sat on a side stool, chewing gum and tapping her feet on the rug. Tim and Chris stood beside Emeka who was seated on a sofa. Pius sat on a chair at the dining table, with Junior beside him. Dorothy stood, fiddling with a lock of her hair, and occasionally glanced at Nick who sat on the stairs looking down on everyone.

"What are we waiting for?" Dorothy asked.

"Who is this? How did you even get into this house, let alone have the guts to be in a meeting with me?" Jennifer shouted at her.

"Because I'm the mother of Chief's son, Emeka. I have every right to be here."

"Which son?" Jennifer retorted. "Chief has no other son than Junior. Your imposter son shouldn't be here in the first place."

"They have every right to be here," Rita said.

"And who are you to make that decision?" Jennifer asked, gesturing at Rita.

"Look, Jennifer," Rita said as she stood up. "You can't decide everyone's fate here. You can't."

"So you have grown up to challenge me, Rita?" She charged at Rita but Dorothy intercepted her.

"Hey! You stay on your end now!" Nick shouted at Dorothy.

"Or else what? What will you do if I don't?" Dorothy retorted. Her outbursts at Nick evidently showed she wasn't normal because Nick's towering size should have frightened her.

"You don't want to know."

"Enough of these squabbles." Pius stood up.

"But why don't you want to listen to others on this issue, Mrs Jennifer?" Tim asked.

"Because there is nothing to listen to. My husband did not have any illegitimate child that I know of. The young man sitting there is not a part of this family. Period!"

"But we have the results of the DNA test that shows he is Chief's son," Chris added.

"What nonsense, DNA test result! Something you can buy from any hospital."

"If you claim the one we have isn't credible, then we can do the test in any hospital you consider reputable."

"I'm not interested and that is the end of it. None of you showed up when Chief was alive, and when he died you come with this nonsense? You know Chief wouldn't have it and I'm not having it either."

"As if you have the absolute right to decide what will happen," Rita said as she returned to her place on the stool.

"Chief knew about Emeka before he died. He asked for this DNA test himself and, in fact, we could bring the doctors who conducted it to talk to this family about it. It was when he was about to bring it to your knowledge that he died," Chris added.

"I suspect she killed my father because of this," Rita said.

"What did you just say?" Jennifer asked and charged at Rita. She rammed into Rita and they fell to the ground, scratching and kicking. Tim, Pius, and Chris rushed in to separate them but Nick, who was closer, grabbed Rita by the arm and pushed her off Jennifer. She hit a flower vase and ended up on the sofa.

"Leave my mommy, leave my mommy!" Junior shouted and ran to hold on to Jennifer, who stood examining herself for any injuries. Two domestic staff ran in from the kitchen and stood by the door taking in the scene. Musa, also drawn in by the commotion, had left the gate and stood at the entrance, mouth agape. The problem was that none of them could decide whose side they were on. They were afraid of their madam but delighted she had met her match.

"What are you doing, Mr Nick? Are you separating the women or joining them in the fight?" Emeka asked as he stood up, looking at the huge figure.

"What does it matter to you?" Nick asked, as he came close to hitting Emeka.

"Hit him!" Dorothy yelled and ran to stand between them. "If you are mad enough, hit him and you'll see madness like you haven't seen before. It's not by this muscles-less fat you think you can intimidate me."

"Shame on you! You are supposed to separate the fight and not join them in it," Chris said, and Tim concurred, but they dared not challenge him to a fight.

Nick looked at them, unsure of who to charge at. He knew he could take on any of them, but he wasn't sure he could take down all of them at once. He regretted listening to Jennifer and not coming along with the boys he had wanted to bring. She had said it would be a meeting with just herself, Father Vitus, and Rita but foolish Musa had let the rest of the bunch into the house when they arrived.

"You have the guts to say this nonsense again here, Rita?" Jennifer asked after she regained her composure and sat on the dining chair beside Pius.

"Is it not the truth? You killed my father," Rita repeated as everyone in the room looked at her, surprise evident on their faces.

"I knew it was you who went to the police with those false accusations, thinking they would arrest me. Shame on you! I'm here!"

"That's because the police decided to ignore all the evidence against you," Rita said.

Dorothy and Chris advanced towards Rita.

"You mean this wicked woman killed Chief and hasn't been arrested?" Dorothy whispered to Rita.

"What sort of evidence do you have, Rita?" Chris inquired.

"Voice tapes, video recording, and pictures," Rita replied.

"And you made a statement to the police and showed them all of that?"

"Yes. I am surprised they didn't arrest her. I think she may have bribed her way out of it, or she has the police officer in charge of the station in her pocket."

"You don't give such cases to the stations. You go to the police division, Rita. How I wish we knew about this earlier."

"What can we really do now?" Rita asked Chris who was going to speak but stopped when he noticed Jennifer had begun to speak again.

"I was waiting for Father Vitus to be here, so we may have a meaningful discussion with all of you," Jennifer said. "But from what I see, there is no need for that. I demand that you all leave my house now."

Rita started laughing.

"I'm going to start breaking heads if you don't leave my house now," Jennifer said, picking up a piece of the broken vase and pointing it in a threatening manner.

"I think we should leave. This woman is certainly not okay," Chris said to Tim.

Musa had come close to tell them to vacate the sitting room.

"Hell no!" Dorothy shouted. "This bitch thinks she's mad?" She looked around for what could be used as a weapon and when she couldn't find anything in the sitting room, she ran in the direction of the kitchen and grabbed a pestle.

She brandished the pestle at everyone, closing in on Jennifer.

"Hold her! Hold her!" Chris shouted. Musa took some steps back to avoid being injured.

"What could Chief have been doing with such a mad person?" Nick said as he laboured, moving himself around to forestall any attack on Jennifer.

"Come! Come and fight, you mad woman. I will let you know that I'm also mad."

Rita fell on the sofa laughing uncontrollably as Emeka ran to take hold of his mother in an attempt to stop her from reaching Nick and Jennifer.

"Jennifer, you think you are mad? You see, we haven't even released our own madness yet," Rita said.

CHAPTER 25

Father walked into the commotion, wondering what was amiss. Apart from Jennifer, Rita, and Junior, he didn't know the others and wondered what they were doing in the house. He'd asked Jennifer to call a family meeting. What was this?

"Thank God you are here at last. Welcome, Father Vitus," Jennifer said, relieved.

"May the peace of the Lord be with you," Father Vitus said, looking over the people in the sitting room.

"Welcome, Uncle," Rita said and went to meet him. Junior followed suit.

While Jennifer was happy Father Vitus had come for the meeting, she was uncertain of how he gained access to the compound without the gate being opened for him. It could only mean one thing.

"Musa, you left the gate open?" Jennifer yelled.

"Oh, Big Madam. Don't kill me," Musa cried and ran out. He was very sure Madam wouldn't let him spend another night after he had let all these people into the compound. Now his woes were compounded. He had heard the noise coming from the house and had run in to find out what was going on, abandoning his duty post and forgetting that he had left the gate wide open.

"I'm sorry for coming late," Father Vitus said, "I went to perform the last rites and offer communion to a dying patient."

"Welcome Father," Emeka said as Father Vitus passed by him in search of a seat.

He looked around, his eyes coming to rest on the broken vase on the floor.

"I hope all is well?"

"All isn't well, Father. These people came to fight me, a widow in my husband's house. They broke into the house and—"

"Uncle, that isn't true," Rita cut in.

"Rita!" Father Vitus said. "Can you let your stepmother finish? Please go ahead." He motioned to Jennifer to continue.

"They came in and fought me and broke these things."

"It's okay, Jennifer. Even if I'm going to say anything about what they did, at least I need to know who they are. Apart from you, Rita, and Junior over there, I do not know any other person. I believe this was meant to be a family meeting."

"Yes, Father. It is meant to be just that."

"Well, Father, Emeka, my son, who is sitting over there, is Chief's son," Dorothy said, pointing in Emeka's direction.

"I don't understand," Father Vitus said, studying Emeka who he now noticed had a striking resemblance to Chief when he was young.

"Let me explain," Chris said as he stepped forward.

"Chief, your brother, contacted me because he suspected he had a child out of wedlock. When his first wife died, he met a woman, this woman here," Chris pointed at Dorothy, and continued.

"She had a son for him and he didn't know about this until recently. Chief engaged my services to investigate this and I was able to get his hair strands and blood sample which Chief took to a lab of his choice where the DNA tests revealed that this boy is indeed his son. He was going to announce it to the family before he died."

"Father, that is not true. They are imposters trying to steal from my husband," Jennifer said.

"You really mean this?" Father beckoned Emeka to come towards him.

"Young man, what is your name?" Father Vitus asked as Emeka sat beside him. "Jennifer, we have to listen to them, and as they have said that there is a DNA test result, I believe we should look at their claims."

"The result is fake, Father. You know anyone can get this sort of thing from any place."

"Why don't you have another test conducted in any reputable hospital of your choice? If the result comes out differently, then you are right," Chris said.

"I am not doing anything. If you didn't show up when my husband was alive, you can't bring this rubbish here now."

"Rita, what did you say?" Father Vitus turned to Rita.

"What does she say? Father, you are asking Rita?" Jennifer said in a high-pitched voice. While she felt her anger rising, she couldn't afford to have Father Vitus completely against her.

"Father, can you ask her to keep quiet?" Rita said, "I'm respecting you and that's why I haven't said what's on my mind."

"Say it, you stupid girl, say it," Jennifer said.

"What is this madwoman thinking?" Dorothy said and was going to confront Jennifer, but Tim quickly held her back. He whispered to her to be calm as it was obvious Jennifer only wanted to disrupt the meeting. She could achieve that and if she did, it would be chimaeric to convene such a meeting again.

"I thank everyone for being here," Father Vitus said. "Before I say what I have to say, may I meet everyone and know what they are doing here?"

Chris introduced himself and pointed out that he was there to give an account of his encounter with Chief. He also introduced Emeka, Dorothy, and Tim as Emeka's lawyer.

Jennifer introduced Pius as the family's lawyer, and Nick as an assistant living in the house who could be considered part of the family. By this time, the domestic staff who were by the kitchen door had disappeared.

"Welcome, everyone," Father Vitus said, sure he understood the role everyone played and why there was a need for them in the room.

"This meeting was called to make arrangements for my brother's burial. I have been away on mission work and I just got back. As soon as I returned, I told Jennifer to call a meeting so we could plan and fix a date for the burial. She mentioned something about the will which we were to look into but from what I can see here now, we have another issue which is also important."

"Very well, Father," Pius said, inching forward. It was his first time speaking. He had watched the unfolding drama, waiting for the right time to step in. He would talk about the will as Jennifer would expect but he was very aware Rita was keenly interested in what he had to say.

"It didn't call for this," Father Vitus continued, picking up the broken vase. "You didn't have to fight and break these things."

"Father, she's the one who started the fight," Rita said.

"Rita, what did you just say?" Jennifer shot back.

"Enough! We can't make any progress if we continue this way. Are you children? Why can't you sit and talk things out?" Father Vitus said angrily.

"You are correct, Father," Pius said. "Father, you mentioned a will. I'm aware of that and would like us to discuss that as well, if we can."

"Yes. You are the family's lawyer. Am I right to believe you are in possession of a copy of the will made by my brother?"

"Yes. I am," Pius responded and brought out a sealed envelope he'd kept under the table and handed it to Father Vitus.

"Is this my brother's will?" he asked Jennifer.

"Yes, Father," Jennifer responded.

"Is this the will?" Father waved the envelope at Rita.

"That is not my father's will. There is another will."

"There is no other will," Jennifer said.

"Barrister Pius, are you aware of any other will?"

"I am not aware of any other will," Pius responded, and Jennifer smiled at him, glad that he was sticking to their script. Rita remained silent.

"Did my brother give it to you?"

"No. Mrs Jennifer gave it to me," Pius said.

"Pius, I didn't give you the will," Jennifer interjected angrily. "What are you saying? You brought the will with you and told me that my late husband gave it to you."

"I didn't. You did."

"Pius, look at me. That's not true, remember?" Jennifer said, wishing Pius would look back on all the things she'd done for him leading up to this moment. How she had sent Nick to look for him, clothed him, paid for his flight to Abuja, had lodged and fed him for several days, just for this moment. She hoped he would think of the danger he had just exposed himself to by destroying her plans. She looked at Nick and their eyes met, each feeling dejected. *I will kill him*, she thought.

"It's okay, Jennifer," Father Vitus said, "He said he didn't get the will from Chief. He has been your family's lawyer for several years."

"But he's lying. He is lying," Jennifer responded, wishing this wasn't happening.

"I asked this because I have heard of another lawyer called Yusuf," Father Vitus said, as he turned to look at Jennifer.

Not again, Jennifer thought. How did the priest get to know about Yusuf? Everything seemed to be falling like a pack of cards.

"My brother called me to tell me that one Barrister Yusuf will call me. He said he is a trusted person, who would call me about his will. Barrister Pius, do you know about Barrister Yusuf? Does he work with you?"

"No, I don't know him," Pius responded.

At this point Jennifer knew she had just one chance of getting things back in her favour. And that was Gozy. *If* he succeeded in killing Yusuf. She had asked him to set in motion an armed robbery attack on Barrister Yusuf and in the process, obtain the will from him and kill him. No one would suspect it had anything to do with the will. She knew the only people in the room who knew about Yusuf were herself and Pius whom she would kill once she got the opportunity. It was obvious Father Vitus didn't know much about him, aside from his name, and that didn't pose any issues.

But why couldn't she get in touch with Gozy? The operation was set to happen last night, and earlier in the morning, she had called to find out how it went, but his number was unavailable. Was it the network? They had agreed he would get in touch once the operation was over. But Gozy could be stubborn sometimes. Perhaps he forgot. She sent him a text requesting he reply immediately if Yusuf was dead and how the operation went. The reply came sooner than she expected. The deed had been done. Yusuf Umar no longer posed a threat.

"I am sure you won't find any will other than this." Jennifer smiled affirmatively, as she looked again at the message from Gozy.

CHAPTER 26

Yusuf Umar had expected a scuffle at the gate, so he was accompanied by two armed policemen. They were with him also in case things didn't turn out well. He had to be certain of his safety.

As soon as they got to the gate, he pounded on it and waited. There was no response. He banged on it a second time. Musa opened the small gate and hissed when he saw who it was.

"*Madam no wan see anybody. She dey busy with people*," Musa said as he tried to lock the gate, but one of the policemen forced it open so he could speak with Musa.

"Ah *Oga* Police, you follow this man?" Musa asked.

"Yes, we came with him and we would like to see Madam. It's important." The police officer pushed the gate farther, letting Yusuf and the other policeman into the compound. Musa stepped aside. He grudgingly led them to the house.

***

The sight of Musa entering the sitting room with police officers startled everyone. A common thought ran through their minds: why were they here? Abukakar hadn't come in yet; he stopped to sign the condolence register outside which he wasn't allowed to sign the last time he was in the house.

Father Vitus was the first to speak, as others were too startled to utter a word.

"How may we help you officers?" he asked.

"Good day, Reverend," Yusuf responded. He stepped in while Father Vitus was speaking. Jennifer froze as she caught sight of Yusuf. He hadn't introduced himself but she was sure he was the one. He was the same man who had given her his complimentary card, the same man who had brought the unsettling news about a new will. What was going on? Hadn't Gozy killed him as he said? He'd replied her with a text message saying Yusuf had been killed. She picked up her phone to look at the message again and her hands trembled.

"I am Barrister Yusuf Umar," Yusuf said. "I have a message from late Chief Onu, who thought it wise to have me bring the news of his will to his family upon his death."

"Are you the one with the other will being talked about?" Father Vitus asked.

"Other will? Is there a will different from that made by Chief?"

"Yes, there is," Father Vitus said.

"I do not know anything about that."

"Do you have the will with you?"

"I don't. The will was sealed and deposited at the Probate Registry by Chief himself."

"Is that so?" Father Vitus asked.

"Yes, Reverend." Yusuf responded.

"That is the way it's usually done, Father," Pius added, "in fact, I'd expected the other will claimed to be Chief's will to have been deposited. I was informed at the Probate Registry that a will was deposited and I thought it was the one I had. It was when I discovered it wasn't that I began to suspect all wasn't well."

"Liar!" Jennifer shouted.

"Enough, Jennifer! Enough!" Father Vitus said sternly.

"So, what do we do now?"

"Is there anyone who has an interest in the will and isn't here?"

"There is no other person. Everyone is here," Rita said. She had secretly notified Tim, who had gotten in touch with Yusuf, informing him of the dangers that lay ahead. He hadn't slept in his house since he heard this and also stayed away from his office. He'd told his staff and colleagues he was out of town for a new project with some clients and would be back after a week; meanwhile, he'd taken a room at Rock View Hotel.

"Then I shall inform you of the date* the will shall be read. It shall be done at the High Court."

"Please, we will want it done as soon as possible. We need to settle these issues and bury my brother," Father Vitus said.

"I shall do my best to make it soon, Reverend. I owe that to Chief," Yusuf said.

"Thank you, Mr Yusuf."

"Thank you, Reverend. Am I right to take it that you are Chief's brother?"

"Yes, I am."

"He told me to get in touch with you. I didn't know how else to get across to you after I tried your numbers and they were unavailable. Here is my card. Kindly send me a number to reach you with. I shall contact the rest of the family through you."

"I will do so. I am sorry you couldn't reach me. I went on a mission outside the country and returned to this terrible news of my brother's demise."

"It's unfortunate."

"It is indeed unfortunate, Barrister."

"I will take my leave now. However, as you can see, I came here with armed policemen. I am afraid there are attempts on my life," Yusuf said, looking all over everyone in the room. "Should anyone make an attempt on my life, be assured that the law will catch up with such a person. Whoever is playing such a game should not forget that the ashes children play with was once a burning fire. If anyone thinks an attempt on my life will deter me from my work, such a person is mistaken."

"That is so sad to hear," Father Vitus said.

"I've said enough. The deadliest dogs usually don't bark before they bite," Yusuf said and left. The police officers followed him.

***

Father Vitus had had enough. As Yusuf left, he knew it was time he left also. It had been a difficult task trying to stay neutral in an environment where everyone had something against each other. In all honesty, Jennifer hadn't acted right. She had been the mastermind of everything.

He said farewell to the others and took Rita aside to counsel her on the need to embrace peace, at least for her late father's sake. She agreed, promising not to have further issues with Jennifer. He hugged Junior and promised to give him some toys he'd bought for him from overseas. He shook hands with Emeka and collected his number so they could set a time for the latter to come over to the Parish house.

"Jennifer, kindly walk me out," he said. He would spend some time talking sense into her, if she would listen.

"Okay, Father." Jennifer stood to follow him out.

"I can't believe my brother is dead." Father Vitus looked at the picture of his brother on the wall.

"Sometimes it feels like he just took a trip," Jennifer said.

Father Vitus looked at Jennifer, unsure of what to say to her. He knew he would have reacted differently if he wasn't a priest. His brother's marriage to her was a grave mistake. He had advised against it when Chief told him that he wanted to take a new wife after his first wife died. The fact that his brother had met the woman in a bar troubled him even more. Father Vitus had told Chief to give himself some time to heal, but Chief had told him he was only a priest and wouldn't know why men couldn't stay for long without women. Certain he couldn't convince his brother, he gave his blessings. The wedding was the biggest in town, but his fears had been confirmed.

Chief never complained to Father Vitus about his challenges in the marriage, maybe because he was afraid Father Vitus would criticize him. How he wished now he hadn't been so stiff about it; maybe his brother would have been willing to open up to him.

"Jennifer, you really need to put the family in order," Father Vitus said as they stepped into the open compound.

"Yes, Father."

"You are now the mother and father of the kids. You have to have an open mind about this."

"Yes, Father," Jennifer responded. Though she pretended she was listening, she couldn't wait for him to leave. She needed to call Gozy and find out what had gone wrong. Had he bailed on her? Had he decided to run away and not carry out the task? He couldn't have chickened out. This wasn't the first time he had done something that dangerous for her, and again he had always shown he was committed to the task.

She was too trusting, that was her problem. She had trusted Pius and he had messed things up for her. *I will deal with him later*, she thought.

"Jennifer, are you listening to me?"

"I am, Father," she said.

Someone was knocking repeatedly at the gate. Jennifer called for Musa's attention, but he could be heard mumbling, from inside his little cubicle. He was in the bathroom, it seemed.

"Don't worry, I will get that." Father Vitus moved to check

who it was. Jennifer made to stop him but it was late. He had already opened the gate.

A group of policemen were outside. One of them, obviously the leader of the squad, had been the one knocking.

"Good day, officer," Father Vitus said.

"Good day, Reverend," the leader responded, as he glanced at him and over his shoulder into the compound. Father Vitus used the opportunity to look at the vans parked in front of the gate.

"Is this the house of Mrs Jennifer Onu?" the officer asked, looking first at Father Vitus and then to the woman behind him.

Jennifer had drawn closer to see what was going on. She was trying to find out if she knew any of them, but she hadn't met anyone before. A couple of them were seated in the police vans inscribed with the caption "IGP Monitoring Squad". She wished she could see their faces and also understand what was going on in case it had anything to do with the allegations Rita laid against her.

"Yes, this is Mrs Onu's house," Father Vitus responded.

"Good afternoon, officer, I am Mrs Jennifer Onu," Jennifer said, hoping she could find out why the policemen were in her house, and in such numbers.

At this point, the officer signalled to his colleagues in the van.

"Mr Agada," Jennifer said, reading the name tag on the police officer's uniform, "how can I help you?" She tried to be clement. Her approach was to be polite even though she was petrified and could hardly contain her frustration. She wished she could speak with the officer privately. She would induce him with anything, just about anything to make them back off and never come back.

"Madam, you will soon find out," Mr Agada responded as he looked behind him to his men dragging a young man forward. Jennifer followed his gaze and saw Gozy. He was cuffed, his eyes swollen, clothes rumpled, and he limped.

"Is this the woman that sent you?" Mr Agada asked Gozy.

"Yes, she is," Gozy responded, avoiding eye contact with Jennifer.

"I do not know this young man. I have not seen him before. Please take him back to wherever you got him," Jennifer said, her voice shaky.

"Jennifer, are you saying you don't know me?" Gozy screamed. "You are denying me, Jennifer?"

The noise at the gate had attracted those in the sitting room who came out and stood watching. Musa came out also.

"I know you. I know you, Gozy," Jennifer said, noticing that there was no way she could deny Gozy with Musa, Rita, and Pius present. They would make slighting references to her lies.

"I know you," she said quietly, "But I'm not part of whatever the police said you did."

"Don't worry. You will find out at the station. Jennifer Onu, you are under arrest. You are advised to remain silent as anything you say may be used against you in a court of law," Mr Agada said and quickly a female police officer with him approached Jennifer and handcuffed her.

"Move! Move!" The officer yelled at Jennifer.

"Officers, please, what really happened?" Father Vitus asked, wishing he could just wake up from the terrible nightmare.

"Reverend, I will explain, we should have explained this before the arrest. We are officers of the IGP monitoring unit attached to the police headquarters. Last night, we were carrying out a stop-and-search. This young man drove towards us. He'd thrown away whatever he was smoking but the stench from his car was hard to miss. We stopped him and as we searched his car, we discovered some guns and bullets. We took him to the station and upon interrogation, he confessed that he was going to meet some gang members to carry out an assassination. He confessed that he was sent by this woman to kill a lawyer."

"Jennifer, why would you do such a thing? What has my brother not given you?" Father Vitus asked, remembering what Yusuf had said about an attempt on his life.

Jennifer didn't say anything in response; she merely turned to look at Junior who was frantically calling to her but was held back by a maid.

"Why are you doing this?" Jennifer asked Gozy and started to cry.

"What does it seem like I'm doing?" Gozy said. "I'm not going down alone."

"Wow. Wonders shall never end," Father Vitus said and turned to Rita who sat on the floor crying that she had said her father was killed. Chris, Dorothy, and Pius consoled her.

"Everything will be fine. At least, your father will get justice," Chris said.

"We may be carrying out an autopsy. We would need to have access to the body. I assume you are the late Chief Onu's brother?" Mr Agada asked Father Vitus.

"Yes, I am."

"He has a grownup daughter, right?" Mr Agada asked.

"Yes. I'm here." Rita stood and came forward. "Officer, do whatever you people can do to ensure my brother gets justice. I'm speechless."

"Reverend, be rest assured that we will do our best."

The policewoman led Jennifer towards the van. At first, she resisted but the officers warned they would manhandle her if she did. Jennifer then walked to the van while Gozy was dragged back in his handcuffs. They helped them into the vans and Jennifer and Gozy were asked to sit on the floor of the van. The policemen got into the vehicles, sirens blared as they drove away.

CHAPTER 27

It had been five days since Jack heard from Rita. He hadn't been able to reach her since the last time she called. It seemed she had blocked his phone numbers and blocked his contact on WhatsApp. Each time he called using a different number, she would end the call once she knew he was the caller.

Jack was certain Rita was done with him. At least, that seemed to be the case, but he wasn't done with her. She may have thought that she had used and dumped him, but he wouldn't let that happen.

"Not me!" he exclaimed, tightening his hold on the steering wheel.

He was driving home from the bar.

For the past three days, that had been his routine. Go to the bar, drink heavily, all the while hoping to drown his troubles in as much alcohol as he could manage. How he was able to get home in one piece was a miracle.

It worked, or seemed to work, because once he got home and managed to tuck himself in bed, he slept instantly. That was on the days he wasn't too drunk that he remained in his car when he got home, unable to move. The nights he was totally plastered, he slept in his car, his face on the wheel. He would wake up in the morning with a massive headache and his lingering troubles looming on his mind.

Tonight, as he exited Donatus Onyekwere Road onto the express leading to Area 3 junction, he noted that there were not many cars on the road. The night was quiet and the moon was out. He had left the bar earlier than he usually did and was heading home to sleep, hopefully to get rid of the throbbing pain in his head.

Jack couldn't bear to think of Rita being in another man's arms. He knew she was wild and crazy, but he thought she loved him. He thought they had something good going for them, something that would lead to the altar.

"I can't let her get away with this. I will expose Rita. I will expose Rita," he muttered, as he hit the brakes at a red light.

A black Peugeot 406 pulled up beside him. He looked over at the car. Two guys sat in the front seat of the car. They turned and smiled at him. He smiled at them.

The rear passenger door opened, and two other guys stepped out. Jack was still smiling at the men when a slight movement caught his eyes. When he looked back, one of the men had a gun trained at him. It all happened very fast. Bullets rained on him in quick succession. He let out a high-pitched scream as the men returned to their car and drove off, leaving a note behind.

Jack was trapped in the car, his clothes soaked in his blood. He was shot three times – in his chest, his hip, and his thigh. There was no way he could make it.

He groaned, strength ebbing away. With every passing minute, he became weaker. A few cars had passed and the drivers called him out for parking in the middle of the road. None of them had stopped, even as he tried in vain to get their attention.

After several attempts, he was able to get his phone from his pocket and dial Ene's number. Ene was his cousin who was a nurse at Asokoro Hospital. Letting her know that he had been shot, he could only give a description of where he was before the phone fell out of his hands and he passed out.

* * *

For the first time since this saga had begun, the atmosphere at Chief's house was different. For Rita, it was the first time she felt at home. Since Jennifer's arrest, a lot had changed. Rita had sent all the maids away and reorganized the entire place as she pleased. She gave Musa some money to take a leave and had gotten someone more loyal to her to man the gate.

It wasn't over with Jennifer, and Rita knew this. Jennifer wasn't someone to give in that easily, yet again, Rita was ready to fight to the end. She had asked Emeka and his mother to move into the house. For obvious reasons, she and Junior couldn't be the only ones living in the mansion. Aside from the new maid she hired to make food and clean the house, the place was practically empty. She needed some company. Again, she had seen that Dorothy was rascally; she would hold her close to guard her insanity.

The mansion was big enough for everyone; in fact, the longer she had them under her roof, the more she could exercise some form of control over them. Rita's relationship with Pius was clearer now. He had also moved into the mansion. She often joked that she needed him with her as her lover and her legal adviser. Her man on the outside had informed her that her former love interest, Jack, had been well taken care of. There was nothing to worry about. Things were falling in place just the way she wanted.

At 7:10 a.m., she went downstairs to the central sitting room. She met Agatha, her new maid, cleaning. Besides Junior who was eating corn flakes at the dining table, and Agatha, no other person had come down.

"Good morning, Aunty Rita," the little chap greeted as he gulped another spoonful.

"Hi, Junior," Rita responded and came over to the dining table. She waited to see if Junior would offer her his spoon. He smiled and handed her the spoon.

"Mmmmm, it tastes good!" she exclaimed as she took a scoop.

"Would you like some more?" Junior asked. Rita declined and returned the spoon.

"That's enough," she said and smiled at the boy.

Though Rita despised his mother, somehow she had grown to love the boy. The feeling was mutual as Junior was yet to show any disdain towards her, even when she believed his mother must have told him to do so.

Moments after the police had left with Jennifer, Junior asked Rita what happened to his mother and where the men were taking her. Rita had told him his mother was in some trouble because of something she had done and that was why she was arrested by the police. He had thought she would be back within a few hours, but as the night drew near without her return, he had begun to cry and demanded his mother.

Rita knew the boy loved toys and liked to eat corn flakes, so she had bought him many toys and had instructed Agatha to let him have whatever he wanted. He was only a child; it would reduce his insistent demand for his mother if he was busy with food and toys. She was right after all; her magic worked. Junior was either eating or playing with the toys. It reduced the number of times he asked about his mother. Jennifer had sent someone to get Junior, her sister or so, but on Rita's instruction, the new gateman didn't let the person into the compound.

"Good morning," Dorothy greeted, interrupting Rita's train of thoughts. She was halfway down the stairs.

"Good morning, Madam Dorothy," Rita responded as she turned to look in her direction.

Dorothy appeared scruffy, with most part of her hair ruffled. She wore a nightgown, with a wrapper tied over her waist. Agatha and Junior greeted her.

"It's a beautiful morning. The heat is reducing." Dorothy ran her hand through her ruffled hair.

"Yes. In the coming months, it will get cooler but never too cold. How was the weather in Kenya?"

"It wasn't bad. It was usually humid round the year in Nairobi and the environment was very neat also. I liked everything about the place, except the food."

"Oh. The food isn't nice?"

"They've got all sorts of food like ugali, irio, wali wa nazi. The food is okay, but it can't be compared to our Nigerian meals. For instance, the jollof rice; nothing beats Nigerian Jollof."

"That's true. Agatha, what are we having for breakfast?"

"I'm preparing akara and pap, Ma. There will be tea and bread as well."

"Okay."

"Please, where can one eat ofada rice?" Dorothy asked.

"We can have that in the afternoon. I think Father Vitus asked for that and he will be here today for the meeting with Barrister Yusuf. Agatha, can you prepare it?"

"Yes, Ma. I will also make the jollof rice."

"That's great. Rita, you talked about the meeting last night. What are we discussing?" Dorothy asked as she joined Rita at the dining table. Junior had left for his room.

Emeka came in and greeted the women, who responded.

"The will. Barrister Yusuf said he will come to talk to us about when and where the will is going to be read. Father Vitus said he will let us know what the church's stance on my father's burial."

"Is it in the afternoon? Father said he was coming by eleven," Emeka added.

"It means we have to be quick about whatever we need to do before it's time."

"Good morning, everyone," Pius said, and everyone responded.

"I'm going to get some work done in my room. I will join you later," Rita said and went upstairs.

Dorothy said she was going to freshen up and Emeka left with her. Agatha took her cleaning towel and bucket and retreated to the kitchen, leaving Pius alone in the sitting room.

CHAPTER 28

"Don't move." These were the first words Jack heard as he opened his eyes. Ene and her friend, Dr Franca, sat beside Jack's bed, waiting and praying for a miracle.

The room appeared to be an attempt at a makeshift hospital ward. The IV stand, catheter, and tray full of operating tools had been taken from the hospital.

Following Jack's call, Ene had run into Dr Franca on her way to Jack. She had carried out a cardiopulmonary resuscitation on Dr Franca's sister who had passed out in the hospital the previous week. Since then, she had been looking for a way to return the favour, so she had insisted on going with Ene. They moved about the hospital stealthily, gathering all they thought would be needed for the surgery. It turned out that letting Dr Franca accompany her was a wise choice because Ene wouldn't have been able to carry Jack out of his car alone. Dr Franca also drove Jack's car.

"Where am I?" Jack asked as his eyes darted about frantically. He could only move his eyes, as an excruciating pain shot through him when he tried to turn his neck.

"You are in my house," Ene said and came close so Jack could see her. "I didn't take you to the hospital because they won't attend to you."

"That awful policy of most Nigerian hospitals that request police report before treating gunshot wound. That's terrible. Thank God you are alive," Dr Franca added.

"I heard it's even illegal. It's time lawyers started bringing legal action against hospitals on that," Ene said.

"What happened?" Jack asked. He could feel stitches and bandages all over his body.

"You were shot, in your car. You don't remember that you called me? Thank God you are alive. It's a miracle."

"We removed three bullets. We've been battling to save your life," Dr Franca said.

"Thank you, Dr Franca. Thank you so much for being here for me and my cousin. Jack, this is Dr Franca, my colleague at the hospital. She's the surgeon who removed the bullets."

"Thank you. Thank God. I don't remember anything," Jack said as he made another effort to turn to see the doctor, but the pain wouldn't let him. Dr Franca came over so he could see her face.

"It was risky doing this at home, but we had to save your life. We had to carry out three operations, with two of them being very critical," Dr Franca said.

"You've got a resilient spirit, Jack," Ene said, smiling. "I'm so happy you made it. It's unbelievable."

"Who did this to me?"

"I don't know. Didn't you see them?" Ene asked. "We found a note in your car and I think whoever did this left it. It said, 'I told you, I'm done with you!'"

"Rita!"

"Who?"

"Rita. She is the one that did this. Can I see the note?"

"We can't show you the note now. I can't let you read anything now. What I read to you is the exact content and nothing more."

"That's fine."

"Who is Rita?" Dr Franca asked. "You mean a woman did this to you?"

"Yes. She's my ex-girlfriend. I guess she's more dangerous than I thought."

"That's terrible, Jack," Ene said as she touched his arm.

"I need to find her," Jack said.

"You want to go after someone that did this to you?"

"Yes. I have to get to her because she won't stop until I'm dead."

"But whoever did this won't think you would survive it. Three bullets? One on your chest, almost hitting your heart, one on your hip, and one barely missed your femur."

"I know her intention was to kill me, but when she finds out I'm alive she will come for me. I know her. She's crazy."

"Enough!" Dr Franca said. "We are so happy you woke up but to be candid, this is a miracle. We have performed all the surgeries to remove the bullets, but you aren't strong yet. We only hope there won't be any complications, so don't start nursing ideas of going after someone when you haven't fully recovered from this."

"Imagine someone God saved and he's already running his mouth. That's one problem I have with him. He doesn't listen."

"You have to listen this time. Your life is at stake."

"I get it, Doctor."

"Okay, get some rest. I will leave now; I am on afternoon call so I need to go home and change so I can get to the hospital."

"Thank you, Doctor," Jack said.

"Thank you so much, Doctor Franca. Jack, try to get some sleep, while I walk her to the road to get a taxi."

* * *

Mr Yusuf Umar's meeting with Chief Onu's family was rather

an intimate one. He had used the opportunity to educate them about wills, the processes and procedures, requirements of the law, and how it was usually opened and read.

He said that after reading of the will, an application for probate would be made and this would require the bank certificate, oath of executors, affidavit of attesting witnesses, inventory of assets, and particulars of leasehold or freehold properties as well as the schedule of debts and funeral expenses.

Rita and Father Vitus asked most of the questions and Yusuf responded patiently. Pius had also chipped in a few words.

Yusuf informed them that as the will was lodged at the Probate Registry, an application had to be made to the court for the reading of the will. This he could do, or any member of the family. The family agreed that he should do it.

While Yusuf processed the application, Pius was to work on obtaining Chief's death certificate from the National Population Commission. As required of the law, all interested parties, including Jennifer, were to be notified about the details of the reading of the will.

**

As rumours of Chief Onu's death filtered into the media, every reporter wanted a piece of it. Newsmen and their crew scurried about, digging further to find out the cause of his death. The man was healthy and was seen a while ago laying the foundation for his next real estate project. In no time, the reporters discovered the infighting between his family members and the fact that Chief Onu had a grownup son the world didn't know about. Emeka was in the spotlight for some reporters who were keen on finding out who would take over the huge business empire.

The news of Jennifer's arrest also made it to the front pages of most national newspapers. *This Day*, *The Nation*, *Daily Trust*, and *The Sun* had Chief Onu's picture with captions such as: "Is this the end to Onu's massive empire?" "Oil Mogul allegedly killed by his own family, autopsy reveals".

Some of the business competitors to the subsidiaries under Onu Group sponsored reporters to scramble for more, and so the reporters dug deeper, chasing leads that could put these competitors over and ahead of subsidiaries of Onu Group. It was a strategic war for relevance.

The autopsy had come out and the report was that Chief had died of food poisoning. It also revealed that toxin found in his system wasn't enough to kill him. Jennifer was rumoured to be the mastermind behind the poison in Chief's food, assisted by her maid, Ekaette.

The tape released to the public and which had gone viral on social media confirmed the rumours. She was caught on tape discussing this with Gozy. It was the same tape Rita had given to the police. The question that raced through minds was if it wasn't the poison that killed Chief Onu, what could have dealt the deadly blow that took his life? The police worked tirelessly to unravel the answer but came up with nothing yet.

CHAPTER 29

On the day scheduled for the reading of the will, everyone was seated at 9:00 a.m. in one of the courtrooms at the headquarters of the FCT High Court, Maitama Abuja. It should have been at the office of the Chief Registrar, who doubled as the Probate Registrar but because he was out of the jurisdiction on official assignment, he delegated a director in the Probate Registry to read the will.

Jennifer had been transported to the venue by the police. Emeka and Dorothy were seated together. Rita, Pius, and Junior came together but Junior ran to Jennifer the moment she was brought in. She tried to make a scene, accusing Rita of kidnapping her son.

Rita didn't say anything in response. A police officer warned Jennifer to respect herself and not cause any unpleasant scene. Chris and Tim had also come to the venue and were stopped at the entrance but Emeka asked the policeman at the entrance to allow them into the hall.

The Director of Probate, who was the designated probate officer commissioned to read the will, was already seated at the bench, same place as a judge would sit, behind a large desk at the front of the courtroom, facing the bar. He flipped through some papers, presumably the applications submitted by Mr Yusuf.

"Everyone should settle in," he said as he looked around the courtroom. The court clerk turned on the television on the wall and was testing the audio-visual gadgets.

"Settle in if you are here for the reading of the will of Chief Onu. I am Mr Danlami Ibrahim, a director of Probate and presiding officer for the reading of the will today," the man said. He was bald and dressed in black suit. He hit the gavel a couple of times before there was silence.

"Are the representatives of the families here? Can they please come forward?" Mr Danlami asked.

Rita, Emeka, and Dorothy got up from where they were while Jennifer was led by the policewoman, with her son standing beside her.

"I want you all to see the envelope that contains the will and examine it. You can see that it's sealed," Mr Danlami said. "Can you all see it? It's sealed," he emphasized.

Emeka and Rita nodded while Jennifer remained quiet with a stern look on her face.

"Please, is there any other person who has interest in this will who is not here?"

"I think we are all here," Rita responded as she looked around, avoiding making eye contact with Jennifer.

Father Vitus, Pius, Dorothy, Chris, Tim, and Nick had also drawn closer to examine the envelope.

"Having examined it and as there is no objection to its opening, may I call on the witnesses to the will. If you are a witness to this will, could you step forward with your means of identification, please?"

Two men sitting at the rear of the courtroom stood up and walked to the bench. One of them looked about seventy-five years old and the other didn't look a day older than thirty. The younger man was dressed in *babariga*.

"I am a witness to the will. My name is Juku Ara," he said and handed over his driver's license.

"I am also a witness to the will. My name is Chief Benedict Eze. This is my International Passport," the elderly man said and handed the passport to Mr Danlami.

"Okay, can everyone look over here while I open this envelope?" Mr Danlami opened the sealed envelope. In it was a piece of paper and a tape.

"I can see a tape here. This is the will," he said, holding up the paper.

"And this is a tape also inside the envelope. Nothing else is here," he said, turning the envelope upside down for everyone to see that there was nothing left inside.

"May I please play the tape?" he asked, and received a resounding response that he could. He handed the tape to the clerk to be played using the equipment earlier set up.

The clerk inserted the tape and hit the play button. The image of Chief Onu filled the TV screen. He was seated on a chair in a place that looked like a hotel room.

"Hello, everyone," Chief said and smiled at the camera.

Almost everyone in the courtroom screamed and some burst into tears. The presiding officer rapped the gavel a couple of times to restore order.

"Kindly replay the tape from the beginning." Mr Danlami said to the clerk after order was restored.

THE WILL

"Hello everyone," Chief repeated on the TV screen.

"By the time you are watching this, I will be dead. I made this video to clear the air, knowing how all of you would have turned against each other in a bid to get my fortune. I wanted to have you try your luck first to see what the outcome would be. You may call it a game, albeit a sick one, but it's fun. My life itself on earth was a game.

"You may be wondering what I would stand to gain from watching my family kill each other over my fortune? I don't care because you didn't care either while I was alive.

"My wife, Jennifer, I know you married me for my wealth, and you would do anything to have it. I'm aware of the gigolos you slept with and who kept you company. I'm also aware that you made efforts to kill me, you planned to run away with your lover boy, Gozy, once I was out of the way. You might not know, but I know Junior isn't my son. Despite that, I couldn't put your evil on the innocent boy. I am letting you know now, not that it matters, after all I'm gone, but to let you know I wasn't stupid. I didn't feel like confronting you about these things because I knew you would have denied it and found other means to continue your evil plans.

"My daughter, Rita, you were my little angel until you travelled to the UK for studies and then I lost you. That freedom, or whatever it was, changed you and changed everything about you. I'm surprised at where you got your investigative instincts but then I know that's part of who I am. I was mistaken to think you took after your mother. Oh, she was the perfect soul. Perhaps if she was still alive, I would have been in good hands, and of course, I wouldn't have made the terrible mistake of getting married to Jennifer.

"You became truly a thorn in my flesh, drinking, smoking, and being a nuisance to me always. You could pretend and blend in anywhere you wanted. That was one terrible attribute I had that you got from me. I wish you never did. I know you hate me and blame me for the death of your mother. God knows I loved her and couldn't have caused her any harm. In fact, her death consumed me.

"Barrister Pius, you've been a good and dependable lawyer. I however didn't come to you because I know the troubles you are in and I know that Jennifer would come after you once I'm dead. I know she would influence you to write my will to reflect her wishes. I didn't doubt that you will withstand her, but I know how mischievous and desperate she can be and I didn't want to take that risk. That is why I made this will using a completely different lawyer who I also trust, and will be depositing the same at the probate registry, so it will be seen that things are properly done, and anyone trying to contest this will is wasting his or her time. Thank you for being such a dependable friend, and lawyer; it pained me that you moved to Lagos, but I was glad you did that to save yourself after the heat you generated from the last incidents you experienced.

"Please sit and listen to my will.

"This is the Last Will and Testament of me, Chief Peter Onu of Plot 8 Adekunle Close, Asokoro, Abuja." He paused and smiled into the camera before he took his eyes back to the will.

"PRELIMINARY DECLARATIONS

1. I hereby declare that I have the legal capacity to make this

will. I further declare that this last will and testament reflects my personal wishes without any undue influence whatsoever.

2. I hereby revoke all previous wills and testamentary depositions made by me.

3. I declare that I am married to Mrs Jennifer Onu and I have two children, Rita Onu and Emeka Okoromadu.

4. I declare that Junior Onu, a minor, is not my biological son, as a DNA conducted on him proves so, (a copy of the DNA result is attached here) but I accepted him as my son and treated him as such, as the sins of the mother should not be placed on the innocent child.

5. I hereby declare that this will was made by me of my own volition and I decided to capture same on video to avoid anyone doubting its authenticity. I hope that the beneficiaries respect my wishes and should anyone decide to contest this will as a means of frustrating it, such a person will be made to lose his or her entire benefits under this will.

APPOINTMENT OF EXECUTORS

6. I hereby appoint the following persons to act as executors of my will.
   a. My brother, Rev Father Vitus Onu of Plot 85, Michael Close, Aminu Kano Abuja.
   b. My lawyer of many years, Barrister Pius Egbe of Egbe & Co Chambers, Lagos.
   c. Both executors shall work hand in hand to ensure my wishes are fulfilled.

DISPOSITION OF MY ESTATE

7. I grant as follows:
    i. I give the following gifts to my wife Jennifer Onu:
        a. A plot of land at Egba street, Victoria Island Lagos, registered as 654/FDC/LAS
        b. My Range Rover vehicle with Chassis number 63NB62583
        c. Shares in Hallmark Bank Plc worth N850,000,000.
        d. Ten percent of my shares interest in Golden Home and Properties Plc worth N1,200,000,000
        e. The sum of N53,890,000 being amount left in my Golden Gate Bank Plc with account number 3244476524
        f. My property, a ten-bedroom duplex in Asokoro Abuja, registered as AK23/FDA/ABJ
    ii. I give my daughter Rita Onu the following
        a. Property at No 283B Bourdillon Road, Ikoyi Lagos, registered as 275/BDR/LAS
        b. My Mercedes Benz G-Wagon vehicle with Chassis number 63NB62583
        c. Thirty-five percent of my shares interest in Golden Home and Properties Plc worth N4,200,000,000
        d. The sum of N185,309,650 being amount left in my Home Micro Finance Bank Ltd with account number 2176499092
        e. My property in East London with registration KHI/763/UK
    iii. I give my son Emeka Okoromadu the following:
        a. A plot of land at 904 Cadastral zone, Garki II, Abuja registered as 436/CDZ/FCT

    b. Thirty percent of my shares interest in Golden Home and Properties Plc worth N3,600,000,000

    c. The sum of N232,890,000 being amount left in my Summit Bank Plc with account number 2218880844

    d. All my clothes, shoes and personal belongings to be used by him or set up a family museum for proper passage to my lineage. My clothes and shoes may also be shared with my daughter Rita.

    e. All my books and educational materials to be shared with Rita.

    f. Fifty Percent of my stake in Onu Group of companies worth N18,460,000,000.

iv. I give Junior Onu the following:

    a. The sum of N30,890,000 being the amount left in my GNP Bank Plc with account number 2127662901 which shall be held in trust until he is 18years of age.

    b. The sum of $210,682 being amount left in my Bank of America with account number 87366521 which shall be held in trust until he is 18years of age.

    c. The sum of N232,890,000 being amount left in my Summit Bank Plc with account number 2218880844

v. I give my brother, Father Vitus Onu the following:

    a. My Property, a six-bedroom duplex at No 44 Oronto Close, Wuse Zone 6, registered as 523/FCT/ABJ

    b. The sum of N43,000,000 in Zenith Bank Account with my name and with account number 2299846362.

vi. I give Barrister Pius Egbe the following:

    a. The sum of N89,000,000 being the amount in my Nations Bank Plc with account number 1190988432 which must be used to defray the debts he owes his clients.

Dissolution of the board of Onu Group of Companies.

I hereby request that the board of the Onu Group of Companies be dissolved and interim board head, in the person of Mr Solomon Edeh, the manager in charge of our downstream sector of the company be appointed lead.

My son Emeka Okoromadu shall be made to undergo a compulsory one-year training wherein he shall learn and understand the company management. He shall be made to take over as chairman of the board upon completion of this training. Before assuming office as the Chairman of the board, my son Emeka shall take all the legal steps required to change his name from Emeka Okoromadu to Emeka Onu so as to reflect him as seed of my loin.

My daughter Rita shall be made to also undergo a one-year training and shall resume as the Managing Director of the upstream of the company.

Disposition of the residue of my estate

8. I declare that the residue of my estate be given to Simpliciter Limited and Breath Of Freedom Foundation for the furtherance of their pro bono legal services to indigent persons in Nigeria.

My Burial Arrangements

9. It is my wish that I be given a befitting Catholic burial. I know no one would worry about my burial until my wealth was shared.

I, Chief Peter Onu, the testator affirms that at the time of preparing and executing this will, I am of sound mind.

IN WITNESS OF WHICH I, Chief Peter Onu, have executed this will on this very day.

SIGNED by the within named testator, in the presence of both witnesses

TESTATOR'S SIGNATURE

Witnessed by
Name: Juku Ara
Address: 87E, Ahmadu Bello way, Jos
Occupation: Public Servant
Signature

Witnessed by
Name: Chief Benedict Ogbonna
Address: Plot 19 Margaret Obi close, Off Akintola Williams way, Wuse II, Abuja.
Occupation: Businessman
Signature:

EPILOGUE

The reading of the will took about forty minutes. The presiding officer was quick to get it over with once Chief Onu was done reading his will on the TV screen. He asked that the beneficiaries in the will address him if there was any objection. There was no objection, they all said. It would have been difficult because even Jennifer, who would have contested the will, shelved the idea as the video evidence wherein Chief Onu read the will himself was undeniable. Again, Chief Onu had said he wouldn't want anyone to object to his wishes and whoever did that would lose whatever he bequeathed to the person.

Mr Danlami handed over the will and the tape to the family and requested that the executors initiate burial plans and ensure that the dispositions in the will were carried out.

It was a well fought battle, Rita thought. She would go over her plans with Pius once they got home. She didn't get so much in the will, but she was happy Jennifer wasn't allowed to take everything.

As everyone walked out of the court premises, Rita and Pius together, Dorothy and Emeka were right behind them. Chris and Tim had taken a different route to where they parked their vehicle.

Jennifer, her lawyer, and Nick left before every other person. Led by the police, they took the exit once the reading of the will was over to avoid being questioned by people. She asked that her sister take Junior with her. She would take care of him and every other thing, including getting back at Rita once she got her freedom. If she ever did.

There were a few cameramen at the gate of the court with intent of taking pictures of Jennifer as she came out of the court premises, but they were unaware that the police had taken her out through the back to avoid her being seen. The police were concerned with how much spotlight the case attracted and worried it might affect their investigation. Jennifer hadn't been charged yet, but they got a remand order to keep her in custody. The cameramen, on seeing Rita, scrambled to take pictures of her. Rita stood in full glare of the cameras, hopeful that her picture could make the news headline.

As Rita continued to walk briskly with Pius, a police van pulled up beside them.

"That's her," a voice stated, and someone was seen pointing from the rear seat of the vehicle. Two police officers came out of the vehicle and accosted Rita and Pius.

"Excuse me, what nonsense is this?" Rita shouted.

"You are under arrest, Ms Rita."

"Arrest for what?" Pius fumed.

Jack, who had been pointing from where he sat at the back seat of the vehicle, alighted and approached them.

As Rita turned and saw him, her shoulders dropped.

"I thought you were dead?" she asked, immediately regretting her query.

"Of course, you can see your evil plan didn't work," Jack responded with a smile.

"No! That's not what I mean. I mean..."

"You do not need to explain yourself, Rita. You did your worst, but you couldn't kill me because it wasn't my time yet."

"Who is he and what's he talking about?" Pius asked Rita.

"Erm…erm…he used to be my friend."

"Please move," one of the police officers said. "Move! You have the right to make your statement at the station." The policeman held Rita by the arm, leading her away from Pius.

"Officers, I insist that you can't arrest her like that. Do you know who she is? What has she done?"

"She is being arrested for the murder of Chief Onu, the attempted murder of this young man here, and several other crimes. We have heavy evidence against her," one of the policemen said to Pius as they ordered Rita to move towards the police van.

"What?" Pius fumed, unsure of what to say in response. By now some of the people leaving the courthouse had stopped to watch the unfolding drama as Rita was led to the police vehicle with the cameramen recording the entire scene.

"Get in now!" The driver of the van said to one of the policemen speaking with Pius. As the last policeman climbed into the van, they zoomed off.

The End

ACKNOWLEDGEMENTS

The authors are thankful to God Almighty, the giver of wisdom for without him this book project wouldn't have been possible. We thank Honourable Justice Benedict Bakwaph Kanyip (FNIALS), President of National Industrial Court of Nigeria for his encouragement and support that engineered the writing of this book. We are grateful to the following persons for their editing contributions - Naomi Ekop, Mary Harris, Her Worship Chiemena Okoronkwo, Chinyere Edeh, His Worship Samuel Idhiarhi, Saifullah I. U. Bello, Ashia Godwin, Tope-EniObanke Adegoke, Elaine Imohe, Tega Otevwe, Ify Imohe, Caroline Ebirim, His Worship Abdullazeez, Her Worship Mabel Segun-Bello, and His Worship Mohammadu Munir Sani.

We appreciate the technical team: Vincent Nwaikwu, John Ogueh, Olisa Nnodim, Michael Agene, Olajide Segunfunmi Ebenezer.

We are especially grateful to Hon. Justice Amina Augie JSC, Hon. Justice (Chief) Sotonye Denton-West, (PJ, JCA Rtd), Hon. Justice Hon. Justice I. U. Bello (Hon. CJ FCT Rtd), Hon. Justice Josephine Enobie Ogbeide Obanor, Professor Akinseye George SAN, Mr Y. C. Maikyau SAN, Mr JUK Igwe, Chief Mike Ozehome SAN, and a host of other legal luminaries too many to mention, who contributed in one way or the other to this project.

We thank the board and management of *Thisday*, *Sun Newspapers*, *Daily Trust* and *Guardian* for reading the manuscript and agreeing to write the pre-release reviews of the book.

We thank colleagues in the entertainment industry who have also thrown their weight on this project. To mention a few: AY, Tuface Idibia, Don Jazzy, Zubby Micheal, Mr Macaroni, Brother Shaggi, Davido, Obi Cubana, Okon, Micheal Sani and Femi Babs, Daddy Showkey, Osita Iheme, Flavour, E Money, Rita Dominic, Timaya, Ini Edo, Mr Ibu, Kcee, Phyno, Elenu, Francis Duru, Mercy Johnson, Genevieve Nnaji, Williams Uchemba, Alex Ekubo...

Finally, we say a big thank you to our families for without their backing, we wouldn't have had the relaxed ambience to write this book.